Readers love
Electrify His Heart
by ALANA ANKH

"I adored the story. I got so caught up in it that I stayed awake until 4 a.m. to read it."
—The Blogger Girls

"The world building was great and the setup for the story imaginative."
—Prism Book Alliance

"This powerful and compelling tale had me hooked from the very first page…"
—Rainbow Book Reviews

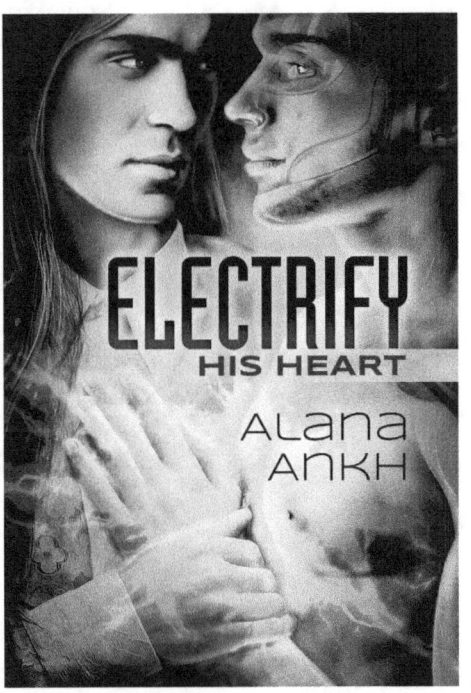

"*Electrify His Heart*
starts slowly, yet soon picks up momentum and then holds the reader tightly until the end."
—Joyfully Reviewed

By ALANA ANKH

All's Fair in Mate Bonds and Publishing
Soul of a Merman
Splat!

ELEMENTAL LOVERS
Beyond the Rift
Fractured Souls

MICROCHIPS AND PURITY
Electrify His Heart
Short-Circuit His Soul

Published by DREAMSPINNER PRESS
http://www.dreamspinnerpress.com

SHORT-CIRCUIT
HIS SOUL

Alana Ankh

DREAMSPINNER
PRESS

Published by
DREAMSPINNER PRESS

5032 Capital Circle SW, Suite 2, PMB# 279, Tallahassee, FL 32305-7886 USA
http://www.dreamspinnerpress.com/

Short-Circuit His Soul
© 2015 Alana Ankh.

Cover Art
© 2015 Paul Richmond.
http://www.paulrichmondstudio.com
Cover content is for illustrative purposes only and any person depicted on the cover is a model.

ISBN: 978-1-63216-981-5
Digital ISBN: 978-1-63216-982-2
Library of Congress Control Number: 2014959930
First Edition April 2015

Printed in the United States of America
∞
This paper meets the requirements of
ANSI/NISO Z39.48-1992 (Permanence of Paper).

Prologue

"HOW IS the process going? We need to have the subject ready soon."

The purist doctor fumbled with the controls on his panel and then turned toward Abigail. "He is almost complete, Guardian Abigail. We are in the final stages of memory implantation."

"Excellent." Abigail would have slumped in relief if she hadn't seen it as a display of weakness on her part. "Make sure you maintain the schedule, but don't make any mistakes. We cannot afford it."

As she fixed the doctor with a stern gaze, Ezekiel slipped into the lab. Abigail gestured him closer to the tank where the Guiding Light's clone was being created. "Well?" she prodded. "Did you talk to the rest of the Council?"

Ezekiel nodded. "They agreed with the plan. The success of Project Uriel proved we can purify our world, but it is obvious that we need to take it further."

Abigail couldn't have agreed more. She had spent her youth watching in horror as the planet grew increasingly polluted with cyborgs, people who taunted nature with their choices. They replaced their flesh with metal and deemed it superior without realizing it was also their Achilles' heel. That was how she and Ezekiel had met, actually, through their shared belief that they could use the high cybernetic coefficient—the percentage of implants in a person's body—of the cyborgs against them. And it

1

had worked beautifully, despite all the sacrifices they'd been forced to make.

But now the remaining cyborgs were getting restless. The resistance was pushing for cyborg rights. Abigail wouldn't have been worried, but her Guiding Light, the man she had created from her own flesh and blood to be the perfect weapon against her enemies—Uriel was proving to be not quite so perfect, after all.

Cloning him would fix part of the problem, but they needed more. They had to make sure the cyborgs were utterly defeated for good, their will and resistance squashed.

"Who will proceed with the implant first?" she asked.

"I will do it," Ezekiel replied. "You have been chosen as my second."

Abigail smiled. It was an honor, and she took it as such. They had once propagated a virus through her newborn, and they would now do the same through their own bodies. She didn't like the fact that she needed an implant for it, but it couldn't be helped. She had done it before, and she could do it again, for her cause.

"The virus is beautiful, Ezekiel," she told her husband. "You should see it. Oh, it will be perfect. Finally, we will have the cyborgs under our full control."

Ezekiel had never been one to show affection toward her. Their love was to the cause, not each other. But now he took her hands and kissed them with obvious enthusiasm. "Indeed, my darling. It will be our ultimate triumph. The cyborgs will never know what hit them."

Neither would Uriel, who would be replaced by his clone by that time. Oh, Abigail could barely wait.

She set her hand on the tank and smiled down at the clone. "You herald a new age. You will awaken to enslave them all. No more mistakes this time. With Project Regenesis, the world will be ours."

IN THE tank, the man with no identity stirred, the words distantly registering in his consciousness. Memories drifted into his mind, the sound of a woman's voice, the cheers of a crowd, the pain of chemicals rushing through his body. Through it all, those words tangled, until at last, they buried deep at the back of his mind, a thorn in his subconscious. And he, Uriel Noah the Second of the House of Zion, slept.

Chapter One

"BREATHE, URIEL. That's it. No, don't slouch. Keep your back straight. Look straight ahead. Oh, dear, why can't you get this right?"

Uriel forced himself to listen, hating the disappointment in his mother's voice. But his head ached, and his muscles protested after an entire day of exercises with very little food or drink. Thankfully, his mother had allowed him to go to the bathroom, because the pressure on his bladder would have added to what was already nigh-unbearable discomfort.

She sighed heavily. "Uriel, you must remember why we are here. You are the Guiding Light. You must show the people that there is hope, their path is right, and their needs are tended to. You are beyond fatigue, beyond physical needs."

As she spoke, Uriel remembered all the people looking at him with adoring eyes, needing him, reaching out to him. He straightened his back and kept the posture his mother had painstakingly taught him. She released a sound of victory. "That's it. Now remember, you must remain in that position. Don't move."

His mother dropped down on a nearby chair, watching him carefully. Uriel kept standing there like she had urged him to. His mind wandered and he imagined himself elsewhere, somewhere beyond these walls, where he could be happy, away from his responsibilities. His mother tsked just as the thought registered, and Uriel started, half-believing she could read his mind. Of course, that

4

was not the case. "You slouched again," she said disapprovingly. "It doesn't seem we can go any further today."

Even with the knowledge that he'd let her—and everyone else—down, Uriel was relieved at the words. It meant his training was over for now, and he could go ahead and take some free time. These intense sessions always exhausted him, and as necessary as they might be, Uriel wished he didn't have to go through with them. Unfortunately, in a week, upon his tenth birthday, they would hold a ceremonial day, and he needed to be prepared.

"Can I go now?" he asked quietly.

"Yes, you can," his mother answered. "Rest well tonight. Tomorrow we must start over."

Uriel wasn't too happy about that idea, but he didn't have a choice. He never did. His birth had decided his position in life, his future, and everything he needed to say or do. He couldn't afford weakness. His people were relying on him to be strong, to be the pillar Edenian society could support itself on. If not for him, their whole world would crumble. Or so his mother always said. Right now, Uriel felt overwhelmed, more aware than ever of how small he was. Tomorrow, everyone else would forget that and rely on him to be the Guiding Light.

With a sigh, Uriel stepped out of the training room and straight outside onto the platform of the Temple of Genesis. He froze in his tracks, every muscle in his body seizing at the shock. How... how could this be? The ceremony was due to happen in a week. He was mentally and physically exhausted and more than unprepared to face his people.

A huge crowd gathered in the agora, reaching out to him in a desperate plea for assistance. Resigning himself to the unavoidable, Uriel walked up to the edge of the platform. He couldn't see his regular guards framing him, but he knew they were there. His existence was too important to the Council, and at all times, he had people watching him.

As he'd been taught, Uriel slid off the ceremonial robes, exposing his body to his people. Not for the first time, he wished he was younger, since during his childhood years, he hadn't been required to be completely naked in front of the crowd. Steeling himself for the grueling ceremony he knew would follow, he gestured the believers to approach.

There were so many of them, low-CC citizens who had survived the virus but whose implants still gave them trouble. Whenever they touched his hair, whenever he came close to them or whispered a blessing, they smiled so openly that Uriel hated himself for hating this. This was his role and his identity, that of the Guiding Light, the last hope of a world torn apart by an unexpected cataclysm. Could he deny them their only comfort, just because of his own selfishness?

As he thought this, a tall man approached and knelt in front of him. At first, Uriel deemed him another believer, but then the man looked up, and Uriel found himself staring into his biological father's dead eyes. Blood seeped out of Ezekiel Zion's mouth as he spat, "Murderer!"

Ezekiel grabbed Uriel's ankle and Uriel's knees grew weak, unable to hold him up. As he collapsed on the platform, he found he couldn't breathe anymore, choking and fighting for air, but unable to draw it in. He tasted blood in his mouth and wondered if he was imagining it filling his lungs. They were everywhere, the corpses, torn flesh and crushed metal, human bones mingling with robotic limbs as they collapsed on top of him. When a pair of strong arms wrapped around him, he tried to fight his way out of the hold, clawing at his unseen attacker.

A strong but gentle voice pierced his consciousness. "Noah, wake up. Come on, baby. It's only a dream. Wake up."

He didn't know which of those words broke through the hold the horrors of his past had on him. It could have been the name, different from the one he recalled in his dreams, or perhaps the endearment that held so much affection and concern. Or maybe it wasn't the words at all, but rather the unfaltering strength of those arms, the familiarity of the voice, and the comforting scent now surrounding him. Either way, because of all that, because he trusted Logan, Noah opened his eyes, stirring from yet another nightmare.

The dream faded, but Noah couldn't let go of it, of everything it meant and how much it hurt him. He buried his face in Logan's chest, crying softly and hating himself for the display of weakness.

"Hush," Logan said, rocking him softly. "You're safe. I'm here."

Noah held on for the longest time, precisely because he believed Logan. He knew he shouldn't cling to his friend this way. It wasn't Logan's responsibility to take care of him, or to mend the cracks that showed up in the middle of the night when Noah could no longer pretend he was a real person. He always told himself he'd stop this, stop burdening Logan, but whenever the dreams returned, his resolve faltered.

Slowly, though, Noah began to calm down. His tears dried, and he found he could breathe a little more normally. "Are you all right?" Logan asked him.

Noah nodded, although he didn't think he could answer. In any case, it was a lie, one he didn't have the courage to vocalize. He wasn't all right. He hadn't ever been all right, because that concept contradicted the idea of his existence.

The dreams were nothing new. He was Uriel's clone, and his creators had imbued him with Uriel's memories. When those recollections came to him, they always created a maddening jumble, a kaleidoscopic mix of doubt, pain, and guilt he could never escape. He took a few deep breaths, struggling to calm his racing heart, trying to chase away the nightmares in that corner of his mind from whence they came. To a certain extent he succeeded, but the shadows of a past not his own only faded away into the background, never quite disappearing.

Finally, he managed to muster enough strength to break away from Logan's embrace. "I'm fine," he said. "Like you said, it was a dream, nothing more."

The raw sound of his own voice surprised him, and he wondered how long he'd been screaming before Logan had managed to wake him. He also realized he must have woken up a good number of the mansion's inhabitants. That guess was confirmed when the bed dipped and a man as familiar to Noah as himself came into view.

7

As Uriel sat down on the bed, he reached for Noah's hand. He'd obviously been waiting somewhere nearby, although his lover, Raze, must have kept him from approaching. It was probably for the best, because they still didn't know the exact extent to which Noah and Uriel were connected, and Noah would have hated propelling Uriel into his nightmare if his brother had touched him. "Noah…."

Noah stopped Uriel before his brother could say anything. "Please don't worry. You know this isn't exactly unusual for me."

"That doesn't make it right," Uriel replied softly. "We have to find some solution to it."

Noah agreed, but he didn't want to burden Uriel with yet another issue. Uriel already had enough on his plate, and some of the things he needed to deal with were of Noah's making. And so, Noah forced a smile for his brother's benefit. "I'm slowly getting better. We're leaving our past behind. The best cure for the nightmares is time."

Uriel's eyes, so much like Noah's own, fixed on his face. He didn't believe Noah—of course he didn't. After all, Uriel's memories remained one of the reasons for Noah's nightmares. Not to mention that they shared a very close bond and, at times, could almost sense each other's emotions. Still, Uriel must have realized he would not get more out of Noah tonight. He turned toward Logan, who gave him a nod of acquiescence. "I'll stay with him. You can go back to sleep. Raze is waiting for you."

The big cyborg was, indeed, waiting, leaning against the wall and watching them carefully with his piercing eyes. Sometimes Noah wondered whether those dark orbs could see all of his secrets, but he tried to keep up a nonplussed front nonetheless. He'd have probably failed if not for Logan's presence, always there, steadying him.

At last, Uriel got up and left the bed. He squeezed Noah's shoulder, but when Noah smiled again, he hesitated. It was Raze who intervened, keeping Noah from having to utter another lie. "Come on, baby. You need to get some rest. Tomorrow is going to be a long, busy day."

With a sigh, Uriel nodded and agreed. "Wake me up if you need anything, anything at all."

"I will," Noah promised.

They both knew he wouldn't, at least not if he could help it. But even if his screams didn't alert Uriel, his brother could still feel him, so his attempts to hide his distress would be futile. It frustrated Noah, but it was likely the only thing that made Uriel agree to leave.

Raze led Uriel out of the room, then closed the door behind them, and Noah settled back down on the bed. Logan pulled him close, slowly petting his hair. They didn't speak, at least not out loud, but the silence between them was thick with unsaid words and emotions that might never be translated into actions. If things had been different.... But no, even that train of thought was dangerous. Logan's friendship was a gift, one Noah hadn't expected to receive. It was the one thing he had, the only part of his life that hadn't belonged to Uriel first. When Logan held him, Noah didn't feel like a broken, imperfect copy. He truly felt like the brother Uriel called him, and it gave him the strength to endure one more day.

Logan also had a knack for knowing exactly what to say under such circumstances. "Want to tell me about it?" he asked. "It might help."

"I doubt it," Noah admitted. "It wasn't any different from the other times."

Logan didn't prod. He just waited patiently, like he always did. Noah wondered how and why Logan could be so patient with him. He'd been deliberately vague when it came to describing his most recent nightmares, but Logan had always stayed with him just the same. Maybe he truly should share it with Logan. After all, his friend was the only man who knew everything about Noah, even his darkest secrets.

"It's just... I was Uriel, back when he acted as the Guiding Light. And then his father... Ezekiel...."

He broke off, unable to continue, but forced himself to go forward. "I couldn't breathe. I felt like... I was drowning."

Before he knew it, he was telling Logan everything. The words came faster as he spoke, Logan's nonjudgmental silence encouraging him, his hold on Noah never faltering. When Noah finished, he found that he felt better. "Thank you," he told his friend. "You're probably sick and tired of babysitting me."

Logan cupped his cheek gently and kissed his forehead. "Don't worry about that. Just remember I'll always be here, and as long as I'm around, no one is ever going to hurt you. Now get some sleep. You're safe."

If Logan had left, Noah wouldn't have had the courage to return to the realm of his nightmares. As it was, he closed his eyes again and slowly succumbed to exhaustion. If he dreamed, he didn't remember it.

LOGAN HELD Noah close, watching his charge's face in earnest. As Noah's breath evened out in sleep, Logan let out a sigh of relief. He hoped that this time around, Noah would finally get some well-deserved rest.

The "choking" dreams had become increasingly frequent as of late. Noah hadn't actually told him about the content of his nightmares until today, but Logan had been around long enough to judge Noah's responses and had noticed Noah's inability to breathe. It didn't take a genius to connect them to the source of Noah's existence, the laboratory where he'd been created as Uriel's clone. While Noah shouldn't have physically suffered from breathing difficulties during the process, his mind clearly remembered the actual experience. Mixed with every other thing that burdened his soul, it made for a deadly cocktail.

It was so hard to look at Noah and remember he'd been genetically engineered as a copy of someone else. Even if, by rights, he and Uriel were next to identical—with the length of their hair being the only physical difference between them—Noah brought out entirely different emotions inside Logan than Uriel did. But then, hadn't it been the same for Raze? Even when Noah had tried to pretend he was Uriel, it hadn't worked. Identical they might be, but they remained two different people.

In his sleep, Noah released a soft whisper. "Logan."

Logan's heart clenched and he ached to reach out to Noah, to truly protect him from everything that could harm him like he had promised. Sadly, he feared he might not be able to. No matter how all of them tried to deny it, Noah was a clone. While that didn't make Noah less of a person in Logan's eyes, it was still a concern. Cloning had been forbidden for very good reasons, and Logan feared Noah's psychological instability might only be the first symptom.

He couldn't blame Noah for killing the Council members. Hell, Logan himself had wanted to do it. He owed them for the death of his family. It hadn't been the right time for Eden, no, but he didn't regret their demise. Unfortunately, the event seemed to have made Noah even more torn, and while Logan had attempted to do some damage control and hide Noah's involvement in it, the consequences would endure, in more than one way.

Noah cuddled closer to him, and Logan wrapped an arm around his friend's shoulders. Noah's hair was soft under his fingertips, and Logan wanted nothing more than to bury his face in it and inhale Noah's scent. Instead, he just lay there, watching Noah and musing over what the morning would bring. One thing was certain. He refused to give up on the man who'd quickly grown to mean so much to him. No matter what happened, he'd stand by Noah's side. He could only hope it would be enough.

Chapter Two

THE IBERIAN diplomat was a dark-skinned woman with black hair tied in a tight, formal knot and a seductive smile that cloaked hidden intentions. The moment she landed in Genesis, she zeroed in on Logan, undoubtedly seeing him as an easy target when compared to all the other members of the Guiding Light's inner circle. It wasn't necessarily very visible. She seemed too professional to display overt advances toward anyone, especially in a public setting. Nonetheless, Noah saw how she looked at Logan, and it made him grind his teeth so hard he feared he might lose them.

To distract himself, he focused on the conversation, clinging to the knowledge of the importance of this meeting. "I'm told that you're planning to create a serum that will help cyborgs all over the world?" she asked.

"Indeed," Uriel answered with a smile. "We hope to be able to give other countries the gift Eden has received. It will not be easy, but in time, we believe it is achievable."

The diplomat hummed thoughtfully. "That's an admirable view, Your Holiness, but if my assumption is correct, it will not be free."

"Condesa de la Vega," Raze intervened, "you must understand our position. Our borders are practically under siege with people we cannot accommodate. We do not have the resources, the housing, or the infrastructure to support the cyborgs who live all over the world. If we were to make this serum a commercial product, it would be out of pure necessity."

"Yes, of course," the diplomat noted. "We understand that. His Royal Majesty is prepared to support you in that regard. We believe cyborgs are citizens as well, and deserve as much care and rights as regular individuals. On the other hand, we do need more information on what this project would entail and how it is possible."

"The project is based on research my brother handles," Uriel answered. "For the moment, the bulk of the information is strictly classified, but we can tell you the serum will rely heavily on my abilities, and his."

It was true that Noah had handled the first steps of the program fighting the effects of the virus on all cyborgs. Of course, at the time, Uriel had been in a coma, and predictions over the likelihood of his recovery glum. Now that Uriel had come back from the proverbial dead, he'd taken over many of the most important duties. Within Eden, Noah's role remained important, but as far as he could tell, foreigners didn't deem him that relevant. If anything, they must have seen him as nothing more than a clone. However, Uriel had set the tone of the meeting from the very beginning, silently pointing out he would not take any abuse directed at Noah. The diplomat was savvy enough not to go against that, but Noah did catch a hint of disgust in her eyes when she looked at him. It quickly vanished, replaced by a more welcoming smile. "I see. I have heard of your achievements, Councilman Noah. I would be honored to know more."

Noah mimicked her expression, although he would have much preferred throwing her out of the room, and out of Eden. "Insofar as it is possible, we will share the information with the international community. For the moment, the serum is still in the early stages of development, and we would prefer to keep the data to ourselves while we perfect the method."

He doubted Iberia would be willing to fund the research based on this promise alone. Even to his own ears, it sounded unsatisfying. He had prepared files with what little information they could reveal, which were to be distributed after they tested the waters, so to speak. Iberia's scientists weren't likely to be satisfied with a few hints, but Noah had no other choice but to risk it. All the data on Project Uriel had been erased, and the secret of Uriel's past had died with the

Council members. However, the knowledge was still there, within Noah and Uriel's genes, and they couldn't allow anyone from the outside to know what they were doing.

It had been hard even within Eden, but Noah had to admit that, for the most part, he'd stalled, unable to provide the real reason why he refused to bring other people into the project. The only person who'd ever seen his DNA was Logan, but they would be forced to bring other doctors in, and that was yet another issue they were struggling with. Because if that happened and if they didn't find an excuse for it, everyone would know Uriel had been the root cause of the virus.

That very same virus had changed many things in Europe, just like it had in Noah's homeland. The centralized European administration had collapsed, as the system that had once supported it could no longer be relied upon. Scared and lost, people had taken refuge in their past to hide from their present.

Some states had remained closely bound, by shared history, language, or geographical location. Such was the case of Iberia—formed over the previous nations of Spain and Portugal. The area had a long-standing tradition of royalty and had fallen back on it, using the ancient royal line as an anchor in these tumultuous times.

In a way, it was sickeningly fortunate that the virus had propagated all over the world, and that Uriel had existed to provide people hope. Otherwise, some lands might have resorted to war in a misguided attempt to return to their former empires—which would have just caused more death.

Still, Iberia remained among the most stable of the nations in Europe, and for that reason, Eden needed their support. Noah kept trying to remember that, but he still couldn't help but loathe the way the condesa's dark eyes lingered on Logan, then piercingly set on him.

Fortunately she didn't push, neither prodding Noah into revealing more information about the serum nor attempting to take her flirtations further. Perhaps she had other plans to investigate the issue, or maybe her king had ordered her not to cross the most powerful people in the world. In that regard, Noah couldn't say she'd been doing a very good job, but Iberian nobles were notoriously arrogant. "Do you have a tentative budget for the serum?" she inquired.

Noah mentally groaned. He did have a rough idea as to what they might need, but the idea of explaining it made his head ache. Currency was another issue that had come up since the abolition of the purist system. He had so many numbers in his brain he was surprised he didn't have nightmares about that too. "At least a hundred thousand gold coins," Noah said, choosing the traditional currency for international trade. He changed his mind at the last moment and added, "About a million credits."

The condesa gave him a pointed look at the elaboration, as if she wanted to say she knew the exchange rate. She held her tongue, and focused on the actual number instead. "That is a heavy burden to shoulder for one nation. I will bring it up with His Majesty, but I do hope you realize we need something more substantial before we offer our unconditional support."

"Thank you, Condesa de la Vega," Uriel answered. "We're in agreement in that regard."

The meeting ended on a somewhat positive, if still tense, note. Unfortunately, the hardest part of the day had yet to come. No sooner had they made sure the diplomat received the best possible accommodations in the new Council headquarters, than the moment came for the second meeting of the day, an even more unpleasant one, if it was possible.

Logan had warned Noah it might be best to sit this one out, but Noah had decided he could not display weakness or hint that he had anything to hide. Therefore, when Uriel, Raze, and Logan entered the meeting room where Abraham Zion waited, he proudly followed, keeping a calm demeanor, even if deep inside, he felt anything but calm.

Distantly related to Uriel's father, Ezekiel, Abraham was the governor of the city of Zion, a settlement founded by Uriel's biological family. Predictably, the purist loyalists in the area, including Abraham, hadn't been happy about the news of the former Council members' deaths. This wasn't the first of the meetings held to pacify the people, and it likely wouldn't be the last.

"What happened, Your Holiness?" Abraham asked without preamble, not even bothering to acknowledge anyone in the room save for Uriel. "How did they die?"

"The cause seems to have been a freak accident at the facility where they were held," Raze replied, speaking in Uriel's stead as they all sat down. "We're investigating the matter more thoroughly, but so far we've found no trace of foul play."

Noah honestly didn't know if that was the case. In fact, he suspected his brother must have guessed Noah might have had some involvement in the death of his parents. Then again, Raze might be completely honest in his answer, because Logan had made sure to wipe out any possible clue that would connect Noah to the event, while also ensuring a solid alibi for him.

Abraham wasn't so easily dissuaded from his quest. "That's very convenient," he shot back. "I find it interesting that the night of their deaths, you immediately left Zion."

Uriel narrowed his eyes at Abraham. "And I find your tone and your implication insulting. May I remind you that you were less than welcoming during our visit?"

"Perhaps, but that isn't the reason you left."

Raze snorted. "This is ridiculous and a waste of time. Isn't it natural that Uriel would want to return to Genesis under such serious circumstances? If you deem our behavior suspicious, feel free to bring it up with the other Council members. I assure you they'll have an amusing time laughing in your face."

Abraham went an interesting shade of red. Noah hid a smile, not wanting to draw attention to himself, but too tickled by Raze's answer to fully suppress his amusement. He was predisposed to disliking the entire House of Zion—with the exception of Uriel, of course—and Abraham's behavior had cemented that dislike. Abraham would have undoubtedly said something quite unpleasant, but Uriel cut him off before he could do so. "We have nothing to prove to you, Governor. You've made your views more than clear, and I assure you that I do not appreciate them. When it comes to the deaths of the former Council members, we will handle the matter, not you."

Like the condesa, Abraham had enough presence of mind not to insist. It was foolish of him to even think he could deem Uriel accountable for their deaths. Then again, Noah suspected Abraham didn't plan to pursue the investigation. The hint of suspicion was enough to shake the faith of the people in the new political system of Eden.

The cyborgs might not care about the former Council members. Three-quarters of Eden's citizens had adopted a "good riddance" policy. However, the previous political system had led Eden for a long time, so the factions still loyal to the dead purists would undoubtedly clash with Uriel. The thought canceled any amusement Noah might have been inclined to feel, but he kept up his front, not wanting to let Abraham see his fear. Abraham didn't look at him, but fixed Uriel with an unreadable gaze. "I believed in you, Your Holiness," he said. "Your people believed in you. But you've committed too many mistakes, and when they stop believing, that will be your end."

He almost sounded sad, although whether that emotion held any honesty was anyone's guess. "There is no value in following someone on the wrong path," Uriel answered. "My parents' death is regrettable, and we mourn their loss. Nonetheless, the change in systems was necessary. I hope that soon you will come to understand it."

Abraham shook his head. "With your permission, Your Holiness, I will take my leave and return to Zion. The people are already restless enough without my being absent."

It occurred to Noah that the man could easily be preparing the way for a revolt, or worse, a civil war. So far, Uriel had managed to stop the minor riots that had erupted after the change in political systems, but an outright civil war meant bloodshed and more deaths—something Noah wanted to avoid at all costs. "I will accompany you there," he said, speaking for the first time since the meeting had started. "After all, who better than the Guiding Light's brother to reassure them everything is all right?"

Everyone turned to stare at him, and Noah froze, realizing exactly what he'd suggested. His offer, while well-meaning, involved a huge

17

potential for disaster. If Abraham figured out the truth, the result could be devastating not just for Noah's family, but also for the whole of Eden. For once, his clone status came in handy, as Abraham shook his head. "I don't think that would be a very good idea."

"He might have a point," Logan intervened. "You have a lot of work to do in Genesis."

"I will go," Raze finally said decisively. "As much as I hate leaving Uriel at such a difficult time, it is first and foremost my responsibility to reassure the citizens."

Abraham grimaced, and Noah suspected the man now regretted not accepting the clone, since instead he would be stuck with the cyborg. He couldn't protest again, not when Uriel clapped his hands and said, "It's settled, then. I will make preparations for your departure. In the meantime, you are welcome to stay here, with us."

"Thank you, Your Holiness. You are too generous. Zion appreciates your interest."

Noah wanted to scoff. The formal words sharply contrasted with what Abraham had said earlier. He held his tongue and schooled his reactions, aware that he might not get lucky again if he drew attention to himself once more in an attempt to help. Mercifully, Raze and Uriel swept Abraham away to make arrangements for the trip.

Uriel threw a small smile over his shoulder from the doorway of the meeting room. "Leave this to us. We'll talk later, all right?"

Noah would have bristled at the dismissiveness of his brother's words, but he understood their source. Uriel must have caught a glimpse of his emotions, and he was undoubtedly concerned. In all honesty, Noah felt relieved to not be forced to endure another meeting, or Abraham's company. Therefore, when Raze and Uriel departed, he stayed in the meeting room, still on the chair he'd used throughout the conversation. No sooner had the door closed behind his brother than a migraine started to pound at his skull. He set his head onto the table, groaning.

Logan was instantly by his side, petting his hair in the gesture that by now seemed so very familiar. "What's wrong? You don't feel well?"

"It's just a headache," Noah replied, surprised when his voice came out steady. "Probably the lack of sleep."

Logan didn't say anything. Noah would have bet money he didn't believe any of Noah's reassurances either, and he didn't need Uriel's abilities to detect the lie. In a surprising twist, he picked Noah up, taking him in his arms. "W-What are you doing?" Noah stammered.

"Hopefully convincing you to get some rest," Logan replied steadily. "You have too many things on your mind, and it's affecting your health."

"Now is not the time for me to take a nap," Noah fumed. "You heard the condesa. We need to make some real breakthrough with the serum."

"I agree, but it won't be now," Logan said, already carrying him out of the room. "Don't bother to argue with me. For the moment, there's very little we can do without risking worse things. You know I'm right."

Unfortunately, Noah did know. In a way, it had been a relief to put the serum project on hold, as they didn't have a clear solution for the most serious issue. Even so, he realized that if he tried to sleep, the nightmares would return. He only seemed able to circumvent them when Logan stayed with him, but he couldn't ask his friend to drop everything just so he could watch Noah sleep. Simply considering the idea humiliated him. "I don't think I can sleep anyway," he admitted. "I might as well do something useful."

Logan didn't immediately answer. He walked through the corridors of the large mansion until he reached Noah's quarters. As he carried Noah inside and set him on the bed, he said, "You have to learn once and for all that you're important to many people. So to us, to me, taking care of yourself *is* useful." He shook his head at his own words. "No, not useful. Essential."

Noah looked up at Logan's looming figure, befuddled. Oftentimes, he couldn't understand his friend's logic, or his own heart. In the grand scheme of things, Noah was just a copy of someone better, but in Logan's eyes, he seemed more.

He couldn't help it. He had to know, needed to understand. For nights on end, Logan had held him, and Noah had gladly allowed it, taking refuge in his friend's strength and studiously avoiding thinking about his reasons. But if he continued with this approach, he might start wishing impossible things, dangerous ones he simply couldn't dwell upon.

"Why?" he asked, his voice now strangled despite his efforts to maintain his composure. "Why are you like this with me?"

Logan stared at him, obviously taken aback by the question. "Why? Do I need a specific reason to care about you?"

Noah's heart started to race faster than it did after one of his dreadful nightmares. He'd realized Logan held some type of affection toward him. He'd have to be blind not to notice that. However, he hadn't dared to hope for too much. Now that he'd unearthed his hidden yearnings, they refused to die down and quietly settle in some corner of Noah's soul. He found himself picking at Logan's reply, prodding for a real answer that might tell him how Logan truly felt. "There is always a reason," he said. "You yourself admit that you care about me. But you know what I am, and you're not particularly fond of Uriel."

"That sounds horrible. I've told you before I don't blame Uriel for what happened. He's my best friend's lover, and he makes Raze happy. That's all I need to know." He plopped down on the bed next to Noah and grimaced. "Maybe…. There might be a part of me that will always remember the past, but either way, you're not him. Whatever genes you might carry, you're an independent individual, a person in your own right." He cupped Noah's cheek gently. "What makes me treat you this way? I have no idea. What made Raze trust Uriel when no one else did? Why did he risk everything and put his fate and his family into Uriel's hands?"

Noah's breath caught, but somehow he managed to whisper an answer.

"You do realize you're comparing us to a couple in love?"

"Am I?" Logan's laugh sounded husky as he brushed his thumb over Noah's lower lip. "Well, that should tell you something, although it might have been a poor comparison just the same. No matter what you or anyone else might say, I don't think you and Uriel are all that alike."

At this point, Noah didn't think he could utter one single noise, not even an inarticulate one. He highly doubted Logan was referring to his physical looks. In that regard, of course he and Uriel were identical. But the main problem didn't lie there. Faces, bodies.... That didn't make up an identity. Memories, experiences—that was entirely different.

If he and Uriel could be set apart, Noah would always come up lacking. He was ultimately flawed, a killer, a copy, whereas Uriel remained just as perfect as ever. But in Logan's eyes, that was not the case, because for Logan, Uriel was not perfect. When he listened to Logan, Noah could almost believe he could be... more.

In spite of himself, Noah began to tear up. He squinted, trying to push back those stubborn tears that insisted on falling. Logan wrapped his arms around him, holding him close, and Noah felt both worse and infinitely better, because yet again, he knew he was taking advantage of his friend's kindness. But even the knowledge that he didn't deserve this couldn't stop him from taking what Logan offered.

He'd never experienced true romantic affection, not even through his memories of Uriel. He'd been created with a registry of recollections that didn't include Raze and the cyborg's time with Uriel. Noah had actually been thankful for that. It was confusing enough to feel the weight of being a clone without remembering romantic emotions not his own.

He'd tried to pretend the relationship between him and Logan was that of close friends and nothing more, but he couldn't hide what he felt. It was selfish, since he had nothing to offer to Logan, but he leaned against the other man's chest, accepting the comfort, but also reveling in Logan's familiar heat.

Logan stroked his hair, and he was so gentle, far gentler than Noah probably deserved. He tangled his fingers in Noah's long hair, not trying to shush him, simply being there, giving him silent comfort. And even if the hold was only meant to be soothing, Noah's body responded in a different way.

21

He knew he shouldn't do it. It was a poor idea at best, and a betrayal of Logan's friendship at worst. But still, when Logan pulled away, Noah followed his heart. He grabbed Logan's arm, keeping him from leaving the bed, then pressed his mouth to Logan's.

The kiss was awkward, close-mouthed, not quite the experience Noah had expected. He'd never kissed anyone before— well, not like a lover, since he had kissed Uriel's cheek a handful of times—but he had been staring at Logan's lips for quite a while, wondering how they'd feel, how Logan's mouth would taste. When he realized he hadn't planned anything beyond this point, he panicked and would have pulled away. Before he could do so, Logan responded, or rather, he took over. The kiss went from being a clumsy clash of lips initiated by Noah to Logan devouring him, exploring him, tasting him with greed. At first, Logan licked over the seam of Noah's lips, but when Noah tentatively granted him entrance, Logan thrust his tongue inside. As he did so, he pinned Noah against the mattress, pressing their bodies as close as they could get. Noah felt Logan's erection against his hip, and it made him moan into Logan's mouth. He wrapped one leg around Logan's waist, grinding against the other man, needing the friction, needing Logan more than he did his breath.

And then it happened. Piercing pain exploded through his skull, and Noah went rigid. He bit Logan's lip and reeled away from the kiss, somehow managing to hit his head against the headboard behind him. That only made things worse, and his vision went white. He must have blacked out because the next thing he knew, he saw Logan hovering over him, shouting for a doctor. Noah blinked away the dizziness and reached for Logan's arms. "It's all right," he said weakly. "It's just a headache."

Logan threw him a look, and his dark gaze held both relief and concern. "Just the same, I'd prefer it if a medic saw to you."

Noah winced. He didn't want to see any doctors. Since Uriel's recovery, he avoided the medical wing, because it reminded him of what he was—a thing, a copy. Admitting that would be pathetic and childish, but he still couldn't stop himself from clinging to Logan. "Don't leave me. Don't leave me with them."

"I won't," Logan promised without missing a beat. "I'll be here for as long as you need me."

Noah could have sworn Logan's words made his migraine melt away a little. He wished he could tell Logan to bypass the entire checkup process, but he must have been unconscious longer than he'd thought, because the doctor had already arrived.

"What happened?" Hugh Wells asked as he crouched next to the bed.

Noah squeezed Logan's palm, wordlessly trying to tell him to keep their kiss between them. Logan must have understood, because he proceeded to explain. "He's been having bad headaches. I took him to his room, and well…. He hit his head."

Hugh scanned Noah's face carefully. "How long have you been experiencing these symptoms?"

Noah shrugged. "I don't really know. I get bad nightmares, and I often can't sleep after that. I thought the headaches were because of lack of rest."

"They might be, but they could also be caused by something entirely different. I'd like to do some tests, especially since you hit your head as well."

Noah worried his lower lip, but one look at Logan's concerned, guilty expression made him nod. "Very well."

Logan picked him up with excruciating gentleness, and Noah instinctively set his head on the other man's shoulder. They walked toward the medical bay, with Hugh leading the way, and Logan following behind him, treading slowly, as if not wanting to jar Noah. It came as no surprise when, halfway to their destination, they ran into Uriel.

"Is everything all right?" he asked, his eyes wide and his face pale.

Noah would have said yes, since the last thing his brother needed was to worry about him. Logan spoke in his stead. "We don't know yet. Hugh wants to perform some tests."

"I'm sure it's nothing, Uriel," Noah offered. "You can go. You have other things to do."

"I'm not going anywhere until I know you're all right," Uriel said stubbornly.

"Is Raze gone?" Logan asked.

A shadow flitted over Uriel's face. "Yes. He left a few minutes ago."

Noah knew how much Uriel hated being separated from his other half. "He'll be back before you know it," he said, trying to soothe his brother. "Besides, we'll be kept busy with everything we have to do. You won't have time to miss him."

Uriel smiled tightly, although it was a mystery whether the concern in his eyes came from Raze's departure or Noah's ailment. Probably a bit of both. Noah tried to feel optimistic about the situation, hoping it would help Uriel too.

He couldn't tell if it worked, because they soon reached their destination. They entered a large room that boasted a wide array of scanners, including a cyber tube meant for complex diagnosis. Noah immediately panicked. "I don't want to go into the tube."

Hugh threw a glance toward him. "It would be the fastest way to make sure everything is in order."

Noah shook his head so hard it started pounding again. "No."

Logan rocked him softly, shushing him. "It's all right. No one is going to make you do anything you're uncomfortable with. There are other scanners."

"Yes, of course," Hugh said, as if taking Logan's cue. "Please, come this way."

Logan gently sat Noah in a low chair that looked oddly like an old-fashioned chaise longue—or would have if not for all the machines around it. The sight filled Noah with anxiety, and electricity crackled under his fingertips. Logan took his hand and squeezed it tightly. "Breathe. I promise you it will be all right."

Noah realized he could easily hurt Logan through his abilities. All cyborgs were vulnerable to his bioenergy, and while his power wasn't quite as intense as Uriel's, it had steadily grown as he spent time with his brother. Logan didn't seem afraid, though, and that calmed Noah.

Hugh placed some sensors on Noah's forehead, on his wrists and his chest. Noah closed his eyes, focusing on the heat of Logan's hand instead of what Hugh was doing. His brother knelt on his other side and twined their fingers together as well, and it felt almost comfortable to be here, with the two people he loved most in the world.

They didn't speak, but they didn't have to, because just their touch meant the world to Noah. The sensors beeped, but Noah remained calm. Before he knew it, the process he had feared so much was over.

Hugh removed the sensors with great care but gestured for Noah to remain in his seat. "With your permission, I'd like to also draw some blood and ask you a few questions."

Noah didn't think that was a very good idea. The scanner machine couldn't read his DNA, but with a blood sample, a scientist like Hugh could figure out the truth about Project Uriel. "Is it absolutely necessary?"

"I think so, yes," Hugh replied.

Noah shared a look with Uriel, the refusal still on his lips. Much to his surprise, his brother nodded. "It might be for the best."

It baffled Noah that Uriel was concerned enough for him to take the chance, but he went with it. "Very well."

Hugh approached with a syringe. Noah rolled up his sleeve, and then stared at Hugh's face instead of the needle. It wasn't that he actually feared the pain of what this checkup involved, but it reminded him too much of other tubes, other needles, other medical laboratories which were increasingly on his mind.

"Have you experienced any pain in your limbs, any weakness?" Hugh asked as he pressed the syringe to Noah's vein.

Noah shook his head. "Not that I can remember."

"What about lapses of judgment?" Hugh pulled the needle away, the vial attached to it already filled with blood. Noah hadn't even felt the pinprick, but that wasn't surprising. "Have you found yourself doing or thinking unusual things?"

Noah barely managed to suppress a wince, and it wasn't because of the pressure of Hugh's fingers as the doctor sanitized the slight wound. The memory of one particular night came back in vivid detail, and with it, the remorse that made his stomach roil. He hadn't wanted to let the previous Council members get away with what they'd done. But he knew now that his brutal solution had been a bad idea. It made him as cruel as them, and it had caused more problems than it had solved.

He was afraid he'd let something slip by his moment of pause, but Uriel intervened before Hugh could notice anything. "Mr. Wells, Noah and I have had an unpleasant upbringing. Both of us often think unusual things."

"Yes, of course," the doctor said quickly as he labeled the vial of blood and placed it in a safe container. "But you must understand, I need the information to better pinpoint your brother's condition."

"Do nightmares count?" Noah asked, surprised his voice didn't shake. "They're very vivid."

Hugh hummed thoughtfully. "Anything in particular that stands out?"

Noah hesitated, and the doctor must have noticed. "I realize that this is a very private question, and I am not licensed in psychotherapy. But I do promise you can count on my discretion, and I have a good reason for asking."

Noah licked his suddenly dry lips. He didn't like to think about his nightmares, but beyond the guilt that stood out from those episodes, something did occur to him. "I... I keep feeling like I'm drowning. But that's not an unusual dream, is it?"

"No, it isn't," the doctor replied absently. He didn't seem convinced of his own words. "Tell you what. I'll prescribe a light herbal remedy that should help you sleep. I'll process the blood tests, and then we'll know if there's something more going on, or if this is a natural consequence of your life as the Guiding Light."

Noah scowled. "You don't think that's it, do you?"

Hugh shook his head. "I really couldn't say. I have a theory, but it would be irresponsible of me to present it before I have any real basis for it. Rest for now. I promise I will let you know when I find out more."

Noah didn't like to be kept in the dark, especially not when it came to his own health, and the fact that the doctor presumed to do so annoyed him. But suddenly, he felt so very tired. He wanted nothing more than to go back to his room and sleep in Logan's arms.

"Okay," he mumbled.

Uriel was visibly surprised that he'd agreed, but Logan took that simple word as an invitation. He picked Noah back up, once more demonstrating a strength that under different circumstances would have aroused Noah. "I'll take you to your room, baby."

The words weren't meant as a statement, but as a request for permission. Noah nodded against Logan's shoulder. Logan was saying something else to Uriel and Hugh, but Noah couldn't register it anymore. And then they were leaving the room, Logan murmuring sweet, incomprehensible whispers that Noah could hear but not really process.

Once in Noah's room, Logan gently placed Noah on the bed, and some of the grogginess disappeared from Noah's mind. "Stay with me," he said when Logan pulled away, much like he had earlier.

Logan stared at Noah, a questioning yet undecipherable expression on his face. Just when Noah thought Logan would refuse, the man nodded. "Okay."

They slid under the covers still dressed, having only taken their shoes off. Noah cuddled close to Logan's chest and closed his eyes. He didn't remember falling asleep.

Chapter Three

THE SOUND of the knock at the door startled Logan from his slumber. He hadn't meant to doze off, but holding Noah felt so right, familiar, and comfortable that despite his concern, he'd succumbed to his fatigue. Noah himself was still sleeping, and Logan carefully slid from under the covers, paying close attention so as not to disturb the beautiful young man.

He had no idea at what point Noah had wormed his way into his heart. Perhaps it was from the moment he'd first met Noah's eyes, so much like Uriel's, yet so different. He didn't know. The only thing he felt certain of was that for the first time in his life, he had someone he loved with absolute abandon. He was honest enough with himself to admit that, and to admit his own fears.

He padded to the door, half-hoping it was just Uriel come to check up on his brother. He couldn't say it surprised him to find Hugh on the other side. The doctor was nothing if not efficient. For years, he'd been unable to practice medicine because of the damage the so-called virus had done, but now, with Uriel's help, he'd recovered, and he seemed intent on compensating for all the time he'd lost.

Logan was thankful for Hugh's dedication, but he didn't like the expression on the other man's face. "Are the tests completed already?"

Hugh stole a look past Logan's shoulder. "Is he asleep?"

"Yes. Should I wake him?"

Hugh hesitated, and then shook his head. "I'm not sure it's the best idea for him to hear this."

Terror pooled into Logan's stomach. He tried to tell himself it couldn't be as bad as he imagined, that he was jumping at shadows. Taking a deep breath, he stepped out of the room and closed the door behind himself. The corridor was fortunately empty, and they could talk without risking being overheard. "Well? Tell me."

"I will be blunt. We all know that despite Uriel calling Noah his brother, Noah is in fact his clone." Logan opened his mouth to snap at the doctor, but Hugh lifted his hand. "Please, let me finish. I am not dismissing Noah's worth. It is merely a fact that all of us must know and accept."

Logan clenched his fists and nodded. "Go on."

"I'm sure you know where I'm going with this. From the moment I heard about the cloning, I feared something would happen. Cloning was outlawed for a reason. You might not remember, since it was before your time, but clones were both physically and mentally unstable. I had hoped that the specificity of the Guiding Light's bioenergy would prevent the horror of what happened in the past, but it seems that I was right in being worried."

Logan could barely breathe anymore. He couldn't say he was surprised. In his heart, he had known this was a possibility. But that didn't make it any easier to hear. "Just... stop stalling. Tell me the truth."

"I ran over Noah's scans and compared his blood tests with a sample I took from his brother. The DNA is... peculiar, but I spoke with the Guiding Light, and I'm told it's normal for them."

Logan couldn't quite read Hugh's tone, and he wondered if Hugh had figured out the truth, just like Logan had. If so, he didn't say it, and Logan suspected Uriel's conversation with Hugh had been a little more complex than the doctor let on.

He waited for Hugh to elaborate, and the man did, perhaps realizing that Logan had been aware of the issue with the DNA of the brothers. "There are clear differences between the two sets of blood samples. In the past, clones have encountered serious issues of cellular degeneration, DNA damage, or mutation. Noah seems in the very first stages of this process."

Logan had to lean against the wall so he wouldn't fall over. "So what does that mean for him?"

"It depends, and it varies from case to case. He might have psychotic episodes. It doesn't always happen, but with the history of the Guiding Light, I wouldn't be surprised. I expect a weakening of his immune system, perhaps cachexia—that is, weight loss, muscle atrophy, eventual emaciation. In any case, it is too soon to tell, and his particularities make it impossible to predict." He paused. "They also make him dangerous."

Logan pinned the doctor with a furious look. "You're telling me Noah is sick with a potentially lethal illness and at the same time, you're throwing around accusations?"

"It's not an accusation, Logan, it's fact." Hugh sighed. "This is not the time or the place to discuss it, but you know what I mean. I don't blame them, for any of it, but the fact remains that the power they wield could prove harmful if it got out of control, especially taking into account all the cyborgs who live here."

So Hugh did know. Uriel must have seen what was happening too if he'd agreed to reveal the truth to the doctor. Worse, Logan didn't have any counter to Hugh's words. The doctor was right. Logan didn't fear Noah and never would, but not everyone felt the same way.

"I realize you love him, Logan," Hugh said, his voice softer. "I've known you since you were a brat, and your parents came to me for their regular checkups. We've had our differences in the past, and I admit it was largely my fault, because of my resentment and insecurities. But I do care about you. I have every intention of trying to help him, and you'll receive no judgment from me. But I must warn you that there's a very high chance he might not survive this. And if it becomes too dangerous...."

"We will leave," Logan blurted out before Hugh could finish the phrase. "We'll go somewhere his power can't reach other cyborgs."

"You'd be risking your life. I hope you realize that."

"I don't care. I've risked it before, for things that mattered less. He is…. He is more to me than you can ever imagine."

Hugh rubbed his eyes. He looked like he wanted to say something else, but at that exact moment, Logan's enhanced senses caught the sound of approaching footsteps. He lifted his hand, stopping the doctor. "We'll continue this conversation elsewhere, and at a different time, when we don't run the unnecessary risk of being overheard."

"Agreed." Hugh paused for a moment, and then awkwardly patted Logan's shoulder. "Take care, Logan."

Without another word, the doctor turned on his heel and departed. Logan returned to the room. His gaze immediately went to the bed, where Noah still lay in peaceful slumber.

Logan slid back next to him and kissed Noah's temple gently. The thought that he might lose Noah made his heart clench. He didn't want to think about it. He just wanted to hold Noah in his arms forever, protect him until the end of time, and keep him safe from anything that would dare to hurt him.

In his zeal, he must have disturbed Noah's slumber, because the beautiful young man turned toward him. "Hey," he said with a sleepy smile.

Logan almost couldn't breathe at the love that swelled painfully inside him. "How do you feel?" he managed to ask.

"Better," Noah replied, stretching. "Headache seems gone."

Logan would have been relieved, but he knew it was only a matter of time until the headache returned, or was perhaps replaced by something much worse. For the moment, though, Noah seemed happy, and Logan didn't have the heart to reveal the truth, or his fears.

He brushed a lock of golden hair from Noah's face and smiled. "Still, you should rest some more. You haven't been sleeping well, and you need to recover."

Noah tilted his head, as if considering Logan's suggestion. "Mmmm… I think maybe…. No."

That was the only warning Logan got before Noah pounced on him. Logan reacted instinctively. He took over the kiss, as if they'd never stopped, as if this was a natural continuation of what they'd shared earlier.

Noah tasted sweet and intense, like the bitter chocolate Logan's mother used to bring him and he'd never managed to get quite right in the VR engine. His hair was like silk under Logan's fingertips, and his body moved naturally over Logan's as he sought more intimate touches. His ass rubbed Logan's crotch even as he desperately gave himself over to the kiss. He was beautiful and vibrant and alive, and Logan craved him with a desperation that rivaled even his survival instinct.

But at the back of his mind, Logan was still very much aware that he couldn't have this. Putting a strain on Noah could worsen his condition, accelerate the cellular decomposition. Logan broke the kiss, pushing Noah away. "We need to stop," he said breathlessly. "We can't do this."

His voice sounded unconvincing even to his own ears. It certainly didn't help that Noah seemed to glow with desire, his full lips swollen from their kisses, his cheeks flushed, his hair mussed, and his pupils dilated. "I want you, Logan," Noah whispered back. "Touch me. Take me. I promise you I won't break."

Logan didn't know what it was about Noah's words that tipped him off. He met Noah's eyes, and in their emerald depths, he saw the truth. Suddenly he knew. "You heard."

Noah averted his gaze, apparently unable to look at Logan anymore. "Were you going to keep it from me?" he asked as he slid off Logan. "It didn't exactly come as a huge surprise."

"I didn't want you to know," Logan admitted, "not just yet. I… I don't even want to admit it to myself."

Noah turned to Logan again, and his eyes shone with unshed tears. "Logan, you shouldn't care about me. I'm a foolish, selfish, dangerous man. I shouldn't have kissed you at all, because for all I know, sex between us can trigger some sort of electrical discharge that would harm you. But I did it anyway, because I want to feel you inside me, at least once. What does that say about me?"

Logan cupped Noah's cheek gently. "It says that you're real, baby. It's not wrong to crave things. And when we love someone, it's natural to crave proximity with that person."

Of course, he was making the assumption that Noah loved him, but that was beside the point. He would be content with a drop of Noah's affection, as long as the sadness disappeared from those emerald eyes.

"I… I don't know what to do, Logan," Noah confessed. "I'm scared."

Logan hugged Noah close, trying to contain his own tears. It was so unfair. Noah had lived so little. He had Uriel's memories, but his own life experience had been tragically short. Ever since he'd been created—because "born" wasn't the right word for Noah—he'd worked to clean up messes not his own. He'd suffered and carried burdens too heavy for him to bear, and his moments of happiness were few and far between. And now, this.

"I know, baby," he replied, caressing Noah's hair. "I'm scared too. But don't lose hope. You're special and we have a lot of technology. I'm sure we can figure out a solution."

Noah chuckled against Logan's shoulder, and the sound came out wet and sad, like Noah was crying. "Liar. You're not sure of anything. You can't be."

For all his words, Noah didn't sound resentful, but rather, fond. In a way, he almost seemed resigned. Logan didn't want to hear that. It was far too soon for resignation. He might be in denial, but he needed to cling to hope if he was to remain sane.

He released Noah from his embrace only because he needed to look into Noah's eyes again. "Hey, none of that. You're too strong to give up. We'll fight this."

"You can't fight the unavoidable, Logan," Noah replied. "I don't know why you'd even bother."

The self-loathing that came with the latter sentence speared Logan like a knife to the heart. "All right, listen closely. I'm not very gifted with words, but I have to tell you this, so that maybe you'll understand." He paused and braced himself for what he was about to say.

"I lost my family when I was only a teenager." He caught the flash of guilt that coursed through Noah's gaze and tangled their fingers together, continuing to speak. "Since then, the only people I

33

cared about were Raze and Julian. And then you showed up, and you blew me away. You were a mystery to me. I thought…. How can this be? How can this man stand by Uriel's side when he acknowledges the real connection between them? I thought… if I were in his shoes, I would resent the person I was created after, if only because seeing him sabotaged my own identity. But you didn't, Noah. You didn't resent Uriel. You even agreed with that insulting idea to take his place in Raze's life."

"It was Uriel's last wish," Noah said quietly. "How could I not?"

"You owed him nothing, baby. It was cruel. You know that. We all do. Even Uriel knows, and he regrets it now. But still, you tried, for him, even if it went against your own heart and what you were trying to be and to build."

Noah's lower lip trembled, but Logan went on, because he had to get all of this out, to show Noah how special he was. "You have such an amazing capacity to love, Noah. To a certain extent, so does Uriel, and he shines so brightly that no one ever sees you. No one ever sees your light. But you've never resented him for that. Your soul has a purity that goes beyond anything I could ever express. Everybody else might be blinded by him, but I see you. I always will."

"I'm a killer," Noah gritted out, his voice so low it was almost inaudible.

"You're a man," Logan replied, "and you and I both know that if you'd been thinking straight you wouldn't have gone through with it. But even if that hadn't been the case, I don't blame you. Those people… they weren't even human. They were monsters. And perhaps I don't have the right to judge. I'm a soldier, and I have plenty of blood on my hands. But some things cannot be forgiven or forgotten, and they needed to pay. My only regret is that I didn't kill them so you wouldn't have to shoulder this burden."

"Logan…."

"I love you so much, Noah," Logan said. "I know it sounds clichéd and maybe empty, but it's true. I would say it a thousand times if it made you believe it. I respect Uriel now, but I've never felt drawn to him, emotionally or otherwise. So yes, it's worth it. If you heard what I told Hugh, you must know that."

Noah was trembling now, and Logan feared he'd said too much. He shouldn't have mentioned the death of his family. It was still a sore subject, since for some reason Uriel's involvement in it had twisted into an irrational feeling of guilt on Noah's part. He almost thought Noah would pull away, but he didn't. Instead, he pressed his lips to Logan's again.

This kiss was different. No longer about passion and lust, it tasted like tears, need, uncertainty, but most of all, love. Their tongues tangled sensuously, and despite his earlier resolve, Logan couldn't hold back. He pinned Noah against the mattress with his larger bulk, devouring Noah's mouth as he explored Noah's body with his hands. Noah's clothes were in the way, but to fix that, he'd have to move away from Noah, which was another problem. In the end, he broke the kiss to give them both the chance to breathe and leaned back slightly, admiring Noah's mussed form. For once, there was no fear in Noah's eyes.

"Logan," he whispered again, and in that one simple word, Logan heard everything they'd talked about, that desire he was afraid to acknowledge, all the emotions swelling between them.

He couldn't push his need back, couldn't deny it any more than he could deny those feelings. Even knowing this might be a poor idea, he wanted it too—for himself, for Noah, for everything they might never have. Right now, he wouldn't think about his fears of the future, but the truths of his present.

Slowly, he began to remove Noah's clothes, never looking away from Noah's beautiful eyes. As of late, Noah had taken to wearing more modern clothing, straying from the loose robes of the Guiding Light. Still, his clothes weren't anything like Logan's, which was both a novelty and a frustration. With his focus on Noah's face, Logan was far less skilled at it than he'd have liked. Then again, it wasn't a bad thing, since he'd intended to take his time anyway. As he removed Noah's upper garments—a loose flowing shirt—the flash of emotion over Noah's expressive features almost froze him. He ached to be what Noah needed, but he feared he couldn't, that he'd somehow hurt Noah.

The skin under his fingertips was so soft, like warm silk, and Noah shivered. Logan almost pulled his hands away, but Noah seemed to guess his thoughts. "Don't," he murmured. "You're not going to hurt me. I trust you. I want you."

Logan could hear what Noah wasn't saying too. He didn't trust himself, and he was still ashamed for wanting this. How could Logan deny him when he was more important than oxygen? Hell, Logan could have added filters to his lungs that would allow him to breathe CO_2, but he could never replace Noah. He wondered if he'd ever get Noah to believe it.

Words hadn't worked so far, or had only encountered limited success. So Logan would show everything to Noah through actions. He brushed his lips over Noah's again, a ghost of a kiss, almost chaste, but holding a promise that was building up in his heart. Noah responded just as softly, his lips moving against Logan's, a reply to that wordless pledge. Logan went on to kiss Noah's cheeks, his nose, his chin, and his eyelids. He targeted the shell of Noah's ear, nibbling gently and drawing a gasp from Noah. He swirled his tongue in the hollow of Noah's throat, acquainting himself with every erogenous zone, drinking in every soft moan, treasuring it like a prize and sealing it in his heart for all time.

As he settled on the peaked nubs of Noah's nipples, his soon-to-be lover arched his back and cried out, "Logan." It was both sweet and painful, because it reminded Logan that perhaps, someday in the far too near future, Noah wouldn't be here to call his name in that distinctive way only he had, full of emotion every time. But no, Logan refused to consider that possibility. He'd seen too much death to deem the world merciful, but he'd finally been granted love. Something so beautiful couldn't just die.

He lightly sucked on the tender bud in his mouth, all the while reaching for Noah's pants. They were easy to slide off, and Logan nearly let out a moan of his own when he realized Noah wasn't wearing undergarments. He released Noah's nipple with a wet pop, struggling for a measure of control. It wasn't easy. Noah now lay completely naked under him, his long golden hair spread out on the pillows, and he was more beautiful than Logan could have ever imagined, the ultimate temptation.

Logan gripped the shaft jutting from between Noah's legs, massaging gently. Slender and rosy, it was as lovely as the rest of its owner, and Logan's mouth watered for a taste. He decided he had no reason to deny himself and replaced his fingers with his tongue.

Noah hissed, spreading his legs wide to accommodate Logan. More than pleased with the response, Logan licked Noah's cock from base to tip. He swirled his tongue around the glans, stabbing it into the slit and groaning as the flavor of Noah's precum exploded on his taste buds. When his lover buried his hands in his hair, Logan really went to town. He started bobbing his head up and down Noah's dick, sucking for all he was worth. At the back of his mind, he tried to remind himself to go slow, to keep himself from overwhelming or harming Noah. It would have worked, but Noah started to thrust into his mouth with abandon, and Logan's prized control frayed around the edges. He managed to hold on to Noah's hips, keeping his lover from pushing himself too hard. But even throughout all this, he craved Noah's taste too much for it to be completely selfless, so he took Noah's cock all the way into his throat and swallowed.

That was it. With another cry, Noah came, filling Logan's mouth with his spunk. Logan swallowed every sweet-and-salty drop, suckling lightly until Noah had nothing else to give.

When Noah slumped down on the bed, though, Logan experienced a burst of panic. He hadn't come, but his dick lost interest at the thought that he might have taken things too far.

Doing his best to maintain his composure, Logan reached for Noah's cheek. "Are you okay?" he breathed out.

Noah smiled lazily, and the happiness in the expression almost stopped Logan's heart. "Never better."

Just like that, Logan's arousal returned with a vengeance. His cock went rock hard yet again. Before he knew what he was doing, Logan took off his vest and undid the buckles of his pants. He didn't ask, because he knew the question would only slide doubts between them. Noah wanted this, but at some level, he was still torn, remembering Hugh's words, fearing what his power might do to Logan. Even so, right now, Noah wasn't thinking about that pain. He wasn't identifying himself as Uriel's clone as he often tended to do during moments of depression. He wasn't dwelling on his guilt over the deaths of the members of the previous Council. He was happy, and for Logan, this happiness, this moment—they were priceless and beautiful and everything, everything Logan had ached for.

Noah welcomed him in his embrace, and when they kissed again, Noah held him tightly, like he never wanted to let go. Their naked bodies entwined, and they fit each other perfectly, just like Logan had known they would. Logan wished he had a mental computer like Raze, because it might have given him an advantage in keeping at least a measure of rationality.

In the end, it was his feelings for Noah that granted him the edge. When they broke apart, he remembered Noah was a virgin and if they were about to do what they were, well... obviously about to do, he would need very thorough preparation. "Do you have lubricant anywhere?"

Noah blushed, and Logan didn't know how he even detected it since he was already beautifully pink after the blowjob. "In the drawer. I have some massage oil."

Logan fumbled a little, but he managed to press the button that opened the drawer. Inside, he found the slim bottle of oil. He quickly uncapped it and poured a generous amount on his fingers. Noah lifted his legs, exposing his pucker to Logan's greedy eyes. Apparently, though he might not have any practical experience, he knew what went on between two male lovers.

Of course, theoretical knowledge didn't mean he was ready for the experience. Logan supported Noah's legs on his shoulders to avoid any possible strain and reached for that tiny, pink opening. He rubbed the oil around the rim without actually pushing inside. Noah gasped lightly. He liked that.

Encouraged, Logan inserted one fingertip into Noah's hole. He mentally cursed. Noah was so tight, and his velvet heat made Logan's cock throb and ache even more. But Logan would have to suffer for a while longer, because Noah tensed. "Feels strange?" Logan asked.

Noah nodded, pouting adorably and scrunching his nose, like he couldn't quite decide how it felt.

"That's fine," Logan soothed him. "Relax. Breathe. Accept it."

Noah tried, but he was trying too hard, and it was making his ass muscles clench and unclench around Logan's digits. "Breathe, baby," Logan advised him again. "Slowly."

It didn't work, and Noah was only getting frustrated with himself. Logan met those emerald eyes he loved so much. "Do you trust me?"

Noah nodded steadily, something that humbled Logan even if he'd expected it. "Then let me take care of everything, baby," he said with a smile. "I'll make it so good for you. I promise."

As if by some sort of miracle, all the tension drained from Noah's body. He relaxed, breathing like Logan had told him to. "Okay."

Logan added more oil, and this time, when he inserted the finger, Noah didn't resist. In fact, Noah's flesh yielded to him easily, almost greedily. Logan bit the inside of his cheek so as not to let out the tortured groan building in his throat. He focused on Noah, scanning his lover's face for any sign of discomfort. He found only pleasure, which escalated to ecstasy when Logan found Noah's prostate.

"Oh, Logan…. Please. There!"

Logan complied, aiming for the spongy gland, monitoring Noah's reactions. Despite having climaxed minutes earlier, Noah was hard again, and his breath came out in heavy pants. When he tried to impale himself on Logan's finger, Logan held him back, which made Noah whine in protest. And shit, that shouldn't have excited Logan as much as it did.

Drawing on the same strength he'd once used for military operations, he continued to hold back and added more oil to his fingers. He worked another digit into Noah's body, finger-fucking him at that same leisurely pace. Noah received it with a moan of pleasure.

Distantly, Logan noted sparks of electricity crackled in the air. Maybe it should have made him wary, but it didn't. He kept going, adding another finger and scissoring them inside Noah. As Logan stretched his lover's channel, Noah moved back against him, his rapt expression screaming for more.

An eternity later, Logan decided Noah was ready. He'd taken his time, just like he'd wanted, and waiting more would be counterproductive. He pulled his digits out of Noah and took a couple of deep breaths, struggling to calm his racing heart. It didn't work, so he poured the excess energy into slicking up his cock. His hands trembled and he used too much oil, but he was at his limit, so he couldn't berate himself for it.

Finally, he positioned his cock at Noah's entrance. He gazed deeply into Noah's eyes, and his lover nodded. "Yes. Yes, please."

Logan didn't need any extra encouragement. He pushed, slowly piercing Noah's body. Even if he'd taken his time with the preparation, Noah was still so tight, and Logan's vision cracked around the edges as he struggled against coming and ending this before he'd even started.

As Logan gradually buried himself inside Noah, every inch of his body flared to life. Electricity burned through his every cell. Noah gripped his shoulders hard, his eyes glowing with inner power. Logan knew he was trying to contain his abilities, but he didn't want that.

"It's okay," he managed to croak out. "Let go."

"I don't want to hurt you," Noah whimpered.

"You won't."

Like any self-respecting soldier, Logan had a pretty high cybernetic coefficient. It was just slightly lower than Raze's, and his implants included muscle improvements, additions to his bone structure in key places, and of course, the regular eye implants. He'd lost most of it after the virus, and while that had come with quite a lot of pain, he'd survived better than other cyborgs, and Raze had helped him through his recovery. Now he had the use of his implants back, and so he could experience Noah's bioenergy in full. But despite his high CC, he had no fear, and he instinctively knew that he and Noah fit together so well Noah's power wouldn't harm him. Uriel and Raze had experienced something similar, he knew, and while Uriel's bioenergy worked on Raze, it had never truly hurt Logan's friend.

It might have seemed like a risk because of Noah's instability, but Logan trusted his lover. Noah needed that, to have someone who trusted him. Logan held on to his resolve, and as he fully embedded his shaft inside Noah's channel, he repeated, "Let go."

Noah did, and power rushed over Logan, raw and wild, filled with so much yearning and desire it took his breath away. It didn't short-circuit his implants, but it did reach out to Logan's very soul, as if that peculiar ability was connected and entwined with Noah's essence. Logan remained completely still, breathing through it, embracing it, embracing Noah and loving him more than he'd have ever thought he could love a person.

When he thought he could move without losing it, Logan started to thrust. He continued supporting Noah's legs on his shoulders as he slid in and out of Noah. His lover met his every motion, releasing small "ngh, ngh" sounds whenever Logan hit his prostate. Neither of them spoke. The only sounds in the room were those of their ragged breaths, Noah's erotic cries, and their sweat-slick bodies moving together, flesh sliding against flesh.

Noah kept clinging to Logan's shoulders, but he seemed to be touching Logan everywhere. His bioenergy traveled over Logan's body where he couldn't physically touch, and within it, within this experience, Logan fell in love with Noah all over again. In Noah's unguarded gaze, he saw the same emotions in his heart, the same pleasure.

Was it that knowledge that triggered the unavoidable? Perhaps it was a natural buildup, everything that had happened from the moment they'd kissed, or even before it. Either way, Logan felt the climax closing in, burning over his skin, sizzling in his balls. He wanted to have Noah come undone first, so he reached between their bodies and massaged Noah's leaking dick.

He'd barely touched Noah when his lover released a final cry and came. His ass clenched around Logan's dick. With one final thrust, Logan followed Noah over the edge, overwhelmed with the electric pleasure.

He didn't know how long they rode the wave of their shared climax, but when it was over, Logan collapsed on top of Noah, spent. He had enough presence of mind to roll off his lover before he could squash Noah, and then lay back on the pillows, breathing hard. Noah curled against him, kissing his chest in an almost automatic gesture. "Thank you."

The quiet words made Logan's heart clench, and he held Noah closely, as tightly as he dared. He didn't acknowledge the thanks, because Noah had nothing to thank him for. Logan was the grateful one, because Noah had allowed him into his life, shared his heart and his body with him, given him love.

He kissed Noah's temple with every drop of affection in his heart. "And I love you. Forever."

He didn't expect the words back, and they didn't come. When he looked down at Noah's face, he found his lover's eyes had drifted shut. His chest was rising and falling steadily. Noah had fallen asleep.

Logan couldn't even be disappointed. This was okay for now. For the moment, they had peace. He closed his eyes and resolutely did not think of what would happen later.

WHEN NOAH stirred, the first thing he registered was Logan's heat by his side. Logan's body was like a furnace, and Noah wanted nothing more than to curl up against him for all time. But as memories flashed through his mind's eye, he knew he couldn't afford that luxury. He couldn't afford the forever Logan had offered.

He wished he could have told Logan "I love you" back, but it was a promise he couldn't keep. As they'd made love, he'd managed to forget the truth of his condition, but he couldn't ignore it, not really. And now, what little time he had was up.

His heart heavy, he slid out of Logan's arms. He didn't want to leave, but he didn't have much choice. His power hadn't hurt Logan so far, but it was only a matter of time. Already, he was losing control. He'd killed once. He would do so again, and now that he knew it wasn't an anomaly he could prevent, he had to remove himself before disaster struck.

His breath caught as Logan shifted in the bed, grumbling under his breath. Thankfully, the man didn't wake, although some part of Noah wished he had. He wanted to look into Logan's eyes one more time, tell him what he hadn't had the courage to say then. But no, it would be better this way. Logan would try to stop him if he was awake.

He washed up as quickly as possible, regretting it even as he did so since he wished he hadn't been forced to give up the remnants of Logan's spent passion so soon. True, it wasn't comfortable, but wiping himself down of the traces of cum felt oddly final, like he was letting go of what Logan meant for him. He pushed back the idiotic symbolism and focused on the rest of what he needed to do. Packing took far too long, even if he only dared to grab what was absolutely necessary: a few changes of clothes, a brooch he'd received as a gift from Uriel, a metal hair clip Logan had once given him—which he eventually decided to use instead of placing in the bag. He had to move stealthily, and every passing second posed a risk that Logan would wake. The man was a soldier, after all, and his senses were enhanced by cybernetic implants. Noah didn't know how he succeeded in completing his task without waking Logan, but he did.

He dared one last look toward the bed, which turned out to be a mistake because it almost made him falter. Logan was everything he'd ever wanted: love, forgiveness, truth, a chance for a life of his own. Forcing himself away from him felt physically painful, but Noah did so regardless and focused on the next step of his not-quite plan.

He had two choices, or rather, two paths depending on what circumstances were available to him now. Leaving Genesis would be easy enough, in spite of his conspicuous appearance. He'd just need to steal a hovercraft and sabotage its controls and tracking systems—easy with his bioenergy. However, from that point on, he wasn't that confident. People would soon realize he was gone. He'd have to abandon the hovercraft eventually, and while this land wasn't as populated as it had been twenty years back, Noah wasn't foolish enough to think someone wouldn't eventually discover him.

The answer lay with the Iberian diplomat. Leaning against the command console in his room, he accessed the system, tracking down the current location of the condesa. His heart skipped a beat when he realized she was scheduled to depart in fifteen minutes.

Uriel must have hastened along the proceedings. Anxiety pooled in Noah's gut. It wasn't like his brother to rush these things, not when he knew how important the cooperation of foreign nations could be. Had Abraham Zion caused more trouble? What would Raze find during his trip? Was this solely related to Noah's sickness?

Noah wished he could stay and find out, or better yet, stay and help, but his enduring presence would cause more pain and bring more problems. He grabbed his bags and slid out of the room soundlessly. Outside, he caught a glimpse of the camera and focused on it. He felt the energy flow through him, shutting down the circuits of the device. He'd only meant to temporarily disable the feed, but sparks erupted around it in an alarming display. Noah cursed under his breath. Already, he was losing control of his power. He'd have to be more careful with its use in the future.

The corridors of their mansion were always full of people, so Noah had the worst time navigating through them without being stopped and questioned. The area around his living quarters was more private, but once he hit public spaces, he caught sight of a deluge of men and women heading in various directions. He backtracked, his mind working furiously as he tried to figure out a way to get to his destination.

The answer came when he absently looked up and caught sight of a ventilation shaft. The mansion had been built in an old-fashioned style, so it didn't have the sharp filters modern technology used. Logan had explained it to him once, disgruntled at the hole in their defenses. Any thief with decent tech or set of abilities could sneak inside through there. They didn't have the funding to redo everything, but Logan had proceeded to litter all the ventilation shafts with the latest in cybernetic security systems.

Thankfully for Noah, these systems were not meant to resist a determined Guiding Light, or in this case, a determined clone of him. After securing his bags on his shoulders, Noah used a nearby column to support himself and climbed up to the ventilation shaft. He experienced a moment of panic when he realized he didn't have anything to remove the grid, but then he remembered his metal hair clip. He rotated the screws carefully, doing his best to stay hidden behind the column, not to draw attention, or bend his most prized possession. It worked, and soon, Noah was inside the ventilation shaft, the grid back in place as he crawled through the narrow space.

He was more than grateful he'd memorized the schematics of the entire mansion months ago, because he was running out of time. He reached the hangars with a few minutes to spare and identified the Iberian aircraft with ease.

Uriel was standing in front of it, talking to the diplomat. Noah couldn't hear what they were saying, but Uriel was tense. No one else would have noticed, since Uriel had been taught how to mask his true emotions, but Noah could tell. He wanted to leap down from his hiding spot and teach the condesa a lesson so she wouldn't dare to slight Uriel again. And then Noah caught his brother looking around surreptitiously and realized with a silent gasp that Uriel could probably feel him, and Uriel's tension was likely caused by him sensing Noah's.

Noah took a couple of deep breaths and forced himself to calm down. He thought of Logan's voice, his eyes, his heat. He thought of how safe he'd felt in his embrace. It was painful to have to let all that go, but instead of focusing on the pain, he concentrated on the fact that he'd experienced it.

Beneath him, Uriel responded to what Noah was doing. In turn, the diplomat's demeanor seemed to soften. Whether the change was genuine or not, Noah counted it as a good sign.

Finally, Uriel stepped back, and after a low, formal curtsy, the condesa entered the aircraft that would carry her back to Iberia. Its shape was slightly different from what Noah was used to, boasting curves and metalwork reminiscent of what Europe had been in times long past. But at the very core, the ship had a similar makeup to its Edenian equivalent. Noah slid out of the vent and landed on the floor, the noise from the starting engines disguising the sound. He zeroed in on the side niche meant to open solely when the ship was supplied midflight. It wouldn't have been Noah's first choice for a refuge, but the angle didn't allow him to be picky. It was either that or the garbage disposal units, and the latter option would be extremely risky. The tech involved in that particular process could kill him before his condition had the chance to.

A touch from Noah's fingertips had the niche opening with a swoosh. Noah stumbled inside with far less grace than he'd have liked, largely because the vessel was already in motion. Still, the niche door safely closed without anyone noticing Noah's dash, and as far as Noah could tell, even Uriel seemed unaware of his escape. As quickly as possible, he took refuge in a shadowy corner and waited.

If any guards approached, he'd have to risk leaving the aircraft. Thankfully, it didn't happen. Noah held his breath and kept focusing on happy memories until at last, the Iberian vessel took off. Noah closed his eyes and pressed his hand to the wall of the aircraft. He had decided he'd pace himself when it came to using his powers, but he had to know where they were going, and hopefully, what Iberia planned for negotiations with Eden.

It hadn't been his original purpose for boarding this aircraft, but while he was here, he could at least help Uriel and Logan. He needed to be very careful, because if he got caught trespassing, it could mean war for Eden.

Fortunately, by using the circuitry that ran all throughout the ship, he could reach all the cameras. It was a delicate operation, but both he and Uriel had been doing their best to hone their senses, so in spite of Noah's predicament, he managed. So far, there were no guards anywhere near the niche. Noah forced the camera near his hiding spot to loop past him so the security system wouldn't register his presence.

Once he felt fairly certain he would not be found, he set out to steal a glimpse at the communications of the Iberians. He was not disappointed. He found the Iberian diplomat talking on a huge vidscreen with her king. The conversation was in Latin so he had some trouble at first, but the words soon began to make sense.

"I hate these Edenians," the condesa was saying. "They think they're so clever."

"Do you truly believe they have a serum?"

"They have something, Your Majesty," she replied. "All the cyborgs I met had use of their implants. If nothing else, the Guiding Light's power is definitely genuine."

"We underestimated them." The king hummed. "Have an elaborate report ready for me once you land. I wish to know everything that happened there and why you cut the trip short."

She curtsied. "Yes, Your Majesty."

The screen went dark, and Noah wished he could have learned more from the conversation. Unfortunately, he wasn't as proficient in Latin as Uriel. Like his memories, his knowledge of most everything was implanted, not learned through a steady process. In this, he was yet again an imperfect copy. But even as a copy, he could figure out what Iberia planned, if not from this brief communication, then through other methods.

The condesa set about to write her report, naturally using the console in her quarters. Noah switched the eyes of the cameras for the mind of the computer system. It was a shift that jarred him, and at first, he couldn't quite get a grip on it. He was propelled back into his body so violently that he had to curl in on himself to prevent throwing up. Since the memories had worked the first time, he summoned them now, too, and his lover's smile, immortalized in his mind, settled his pulse and calmed down his impending migraine.

Noah tried again, this time more carefully. He bonded with the computer system far better, and when he found the condesa working on her report, he saw each word as it was typed.

Like the conversation between the diplomat and her king, the report was in Latin. The written words were easier to compute, although Noah rather wished a large part of Europe hadn't decided to use Latin as a diplomat's language of choice. Whatever the case, Noah gathered the information from the report with ease. Apparently, Iberia deemed Eden a potential threat, but at this time, it was not advisable for them to pursue hostile action. Condesa de la Vega believed civil war was imminent, which seemed to be the reason she'd chosen to depart so quickly. Once the internal conflict weakened Eden, she continued, Iberia could sweep in and claim the spoils.

In hindsight, it made sense. Iberia had allies within Europe, but they never would have dared to challenge Eden before recent developments. Uriel's relationship with Raze had knocked him off the pedestal that made Eden immune to outside threats. And while Noah didn't blame his brother in any way for his choice, it was scary to think of the consequences.

Noah could have tried to steal a few more pieces of information, but he already felt exhausted. As the diplomat completed her report, his consciousness returned to his physical body and he took a couple of deep breaths. It once again occurred to him what his presence on the vessel could mean, but this time the knowledge truly processed.

What in the world had he been thinking when he'd boarded this aircraft? Answer: he hadn't. His logical side seemed to have gaps, like the information was there but didn't quite penetrate his consciousness. Or he organized his priorities in a completely wrong way—kind of like he had the night he'd become a killer.

One thing was certain. He needed to get out of here. Iberian guards would definitely spot him if he was still on board when they reached their destination.

It took him some time to recover from forcing his way into the Iberian systems, and it didn't really help that he had to continue keeping an eye on what was happening to prevent being spotted, as well as figure out the moment they'd hit Iberian shores. Hours ticked past, and all the while, Noah thought about the reaction Logan must have had once he'd realized Noah had fled. Did he feel hurt? Betrayed?

Noah shook himself and focused on more practical matters. They were approaching Iberia, so he needed to find a means of safely exiting the ship. Fortunately, the vessel was well-stocked with jet packs. He had to risk leaving his hiding spot to find one, but he tracked down a stash located nearby without being detected by any guards. Noah stole one of the jet packs, paying close attention so the absence of the item wouldn't be detected. Once he made sure that even the inventory in the computer database wouldn't give him away, he headed back the way he'd come.

The capital city of Corduba was quite close to the border, so as soon as he noticed the white beaches through the computer system, he strapped the jet pack on. He double-checked the feed of the cameras and eliminated all traces of his presence, then finally opened the niche door.

Noah had never actually used jet packs before. Every time he'd traveled with one, he'd been in Logan's arms, and the cyborg had maneuvered them in the air. He didn't have that luxury now, and as such, he had to yet again rely on his power to make sure he didn't accidentally have an unpleasant meeting with the engines of the Iberian aircraft.

By some miracle, he landed safely on the beach below. There was no reaction from the aircraft already disappearing in the distance, so Noah decided he must have escaped undetected.

The beach was abandoned, just like Noah had known it would be. It was notoriously one of the places that had been hit hardest by the virus, due to the large concentration of high-CC cyborgs in the area. Iberian beaches had been among the few that had survived the pollutant outburst in the twenty-second century, and it had once overflowed with filthy rich tourists. Ninety-nine percent of them had died on Uriel's birthday, and by the time Iberian authorities had managed a form of organization, the area had become a zone of pestilence and decay.

There was no sign of dead bodies now, after so many years. The beach maintained its beauty, the waters clear and the sand warm as it slid into Noah's sandals. But the heavy silence weighed on Noah, ominous, unnatural. At the edge of the beach, he saw a mausoleum, an elegant column that he knew was engraved with the names of the dead. In the distance, he caught sight of crumbling buildings—the last vestiges of one of the resorts in the area.

Noah shook himself and pushed back the unpleasant thoughts. Suddenly, he felt so exhausted. He had to find a way to contact Eden and warn his brother of Iberia's plans, but he'd overused his powers.

His knees went weak, and he collapsed face-first into the sand. A memory of Logan's whispered "I love you" drifted one last time in his mind before fatigue claimed him and everything went black.

Chapter Four

"So YOU know where he is, then?" Uriel wrung his hands, his eyes pleading as he looked at Logan. "You know where he went?"

Logan looked away from Uriel's face. For the first time, he could fully understand what Raze must have felt like during Uriel's coma. Back then, his friend had been forced to face Noah every single day. Now the situation was in reverse, with Uriel being here while Noah was missing, in danger, dying.

Clearing his throat, he focused on the screen in front of him. "I don't know yet, but hopefully, I will soon. I embedded a tracker in the hairpin I gave him a while back. Hopefully I can use it to detect his current location."

"A tracker?" Uriel repeated. "Is that even going to work?"

Logan glanced away from the console and wondered if Uriel was remembering the other metal hair clip, the one Logan had given him the day they had met. That one had been a simple hair ornament, nothing like Logan's gift to Noah, but there were some things that stayed with people. Sometimes, the oddest details reminded them of the weight of the truths they were both hiding.

Uriel's eyes, so much like Noah's, yet so different, fixed on Logan's face. "Wouldn't a tracker be short-circuited by our powers?"

"Yes, that's a risk," Logan admitted, "which is why it's not active yet. It's also insulated, insofar as it can be, at least." Noah's bioenergy could bypass all the precautions Logan had taken, but

Logan hoped his prototype would work long enough to allow him to get an idea of Noah's location.

Logan held his breath as he activated the device remotely. A tiny light appeared on the console. The system soon produced the coordinates Logan needed and a detailed 3-D map of the area. The Beaches of the Dead. Fuck.

Uriel cursed in an echo of Logan's own thoughts. "Iberia. Of course. I thought I sensed something amiss when I was in the hangars. Dammit."

Logan gaped at Uriel. He'd known about the connection between the two brothers, and he had wondered how Uriel hadn't sensed Noah's plan, but to think Uriel had been within inches of Noah and not even realized it…. It was staggering.

"You've got to be shitting me."

Uriel's shoulders slumped. "I wish I was. I thought I'd imagined it. I should have known better."

Anger coursed through Logan, but he reined it in. Yes, Uriel should have known better, but Logan couldn't exactly point fingers either. Noah had sneaked out from under his nose, and Logan was a trained soldier. He should have woken up when Noah had left the room to begin with. He had no right to throw stones.

"I'm going to Iberia," he said. "We have to find him before anyone else does."

The Beaches of the Dead might be abandoned, but patrols still frequented the area, and Noah could run into one of the groups. Given Noah's condition, there was no telling what would happen.

Uriel's jaw tightened. "I'm coming too."

"Absolutely not," Logan snapped back, wishing they could have called Raze back from his trip. "You're the Guiding Light. You can't afford to leave Eden."

"I can't abandon him. I'm going."

Logan should have pointed out the rational reasons why that was a bad idea. He should have explained that this would be a covert op in a foreign nation, and it would be risky enough with Logan going. Uriel making the trip would be madness. But he was at his wits' end. From the moment he'd woken up alone, he'd been terrified for his lover.

Anger and fear mixed within him, and he snapped at Uriel, "I'll be able to care for Noah just fine without your help."

His tone said more than his words ever could, and Uriel narrowed his eyes. "You can't deny me the right to help Noah. He's my brother."

"You've never seen him as such," Logan snarled at Uriel. "You always look down on him, and you know it."

"That's not true," Uriel bit out. "I made a mistake when I asked him to be Raze's lover in my stead. I admitted to that. But he's my brother, and I love him."

Logan tore his gaze away from Uriel, unable to look at him anymore. In a twisted way, Uriel's presence fueled his anger, so when he didn't have to face that familiar visage anymore, he could fall back onto the calm hammered into him by his training.

"This is a useless argument," he said, hiding his resentment behind his resolve. "You have work to do in Eden, and you're well aware of it. This trip is dangerous enough. I don't think it would be wise to take other people, and me having to watch your back would make you a liability."

To be fair, Uriel could defend himself, and his abilities made him a very powerful asset in any battle. But that didn't change the risks involved in the mission.

"You really think it's a good idea to go alone?" Uriel asked, his tone heavy with doubt.

Logan nodded. "See the dot? It isn't moving. Wherever Noah is, he's probably unconscious." Not for the first time, he wished they could have rebuilt Eden's surveillance satellites, but it wasn't possible yet. "That is the best case scenario, of course. He could have also been captured, but if that were the case, my assumption is that we'd have heard something from the authorities. Either way, we don't have much time at our disposal. If I leave now, I can be there before anything can happen. I don't have the time to brief anyone."

Not to mention that he didn't trust other people with Noah. Even the people who'd come to respect his lover had become dismissive of him once Uriel was back. Yes, Uriel made an effort to include his brother and point out his efforts, but most of the time, it backfired. The only ones who seemed to realize this were Logan and Noah himself.

Without waiting for a reply from Uriel, Logan used the console to activate his weapons stash. The shelves in his room moved aside to reveal his stealth suit and various guns. Logan retrieved the equipment he needed, moving as quickly as possible while trying to not leave anything essential out. It wouldn't do to forget something important because he was in such a hurry.

The door swooshed as Uriel left the room, giving Logan privacy. Logan counted himself lucky for small miracles and changed into his stealth suit. It had gotten him out of various predicaments many times in the past. He had no doubt it would serve him well.

It took a good couple of minutes to make sure the suit connected properly to his neural pathways and his implants. He hadn't worn it for a while now, and he had upgraded it since then. The delay that unavoidably came from the necessary adjustments irritated him.

It didn't help that when he finally left the room, he found Uriel waiting outside. He had hoped the man would just trust him on this one, but apparently that was too much to ask for.

Logan started to walk toward the hangars, with Uriel following behind him. "I know you hate me, Logan," Uriel said quietly, "but…."

Logan stopped midstride and pivoted on his heel, glaring at his pursuer. "Here's what you don't understand, Uriel. This isn't about you. What do you want me to say? That I've forgotten what you are and why you came into being? I haven't, but I also can't hate someone with Noah's face. And I do understand none of it was truly your fault. But that doesn't matter right now. Noah is the only one who matters."

"Yes, I agree," Uriel replied.

"Do you? Because it definitely doesn't seem like it."

Uriel's eyes lit up with a sort of inner flare, and the lights in the corridor flickered. "Logan, I'm tired of this argument. You think I don't care about Noah, and maybe I understand why that is. And some things cannot be set aside, no matter how hard we try.

But I also know Noah. I know his mind and his heart. I feel him. And yes, I have failed him in the past. I should have been there for him more than I was. But that doesn't change the fact that we're in this together, and I want to help him as much as you do." The light steadied, and Uriel stepped back. "You're right. I can't leave Eden. You have to go after him. But I'll encourage the research on Noah's condition while you're gone. And keep me posted, Logan. Please."

Logan nodded jerkily. There was nothing more that could be said. The scar of his family's death was still there, and while he intellectually realized Uriel wasn't to blame, at some level he still saw Uriel as the cause of all that pain. Paradoxically, much like he had told Noah, Logan didn't hate Uriel and in fact was grateful to him for giving Raze a chance at love. However, his frustration over Noah's situation embittered him even more. In this, though, they were allies, and Logan had to let go of old grudges.

"I'll bring him back," he promised. "I'll help him."

Uriel said nothing more, and when Logan started walking again, the other man didn't follow. It was a vote of confidence, and Logan hoped he would be able to keep his promise, if not for Uriel's sake, for Noah's.

No one questioned him as he threw himself into the fastest stealth hovercraft they had, his bag next to him. Perhaps they thought Raze needed backup, and Logan was going to help him out. But today, Logan had his own mission, one he would not fail.

Despite the speed of the specialized hovercraft, the flight over the ocean took far longer than Logan would have liked. As he piloted the aircraft, Logan kept monitoring the tracker, but it didn't move from its previous spot. Logan half-thought Noah might have dropped the hairpin, but if that was the case, Logan would track him down from there. And if someone had indeed taken him, they would pay the price.

Of course, should such a situation come up, Eden itself would have other problems, but Logan had to believe that wasn't the case. If Iberian forces had captured Noah, not even Logan's stealth hovercraft and suit—which had helped him sneak in and out of enemy territory more than once—would allow him to avoid detection.

As it turned out, he needn't have worried, at least, not about finding Noah. He spotted his lover's prone form the moment he came within view of the Beaches of the Dead. His blood froze in his veins at the sight of Noah's still body, and he had the stray, horrifying thought that Noah might have become yet another unfortunate soul who'd come here to die.

He didn't know how he managed to land the hovercraft without crashing it into the sand. It was probably only his training that kept him from doing something stupid, anchoring him until he set the aircraft down and made sure the stealth module would hold in his absence. Still, he practically stumbled out of it in his haste to get to Noah's side.

Logan dropped to his knees next to Noah and turned his lover on his back. He noted Noah wasn't hurt, at least not seriously. He seemed to be out cold, but there were no signs of trauma or other injury. In fact, the moment Logan touched him, Noah cracked his eyes open. "Logan? W-What happened?"

The tight fist clenched around Logan's heart loosened a little. "You don't remember?"

Noah blinked and looked around. Logan regretted his questions when realization dawned in Noah's eyes, and his lover tried to scuttle away. "You shouldn't have come. I left Eden for a reason."

"I know you did, baby," Logan replied, already reaching for him, "but you don't have to be alone. Please, come home."

Noah shook his head adamantly. "I know you mean well, but I'm dangerous. You heard what Doctor Wells said. I could hurt people with my powers. I could hurt you."

Not for the first time, Logan wished he hadn't relied on the closed door to keep Noah from the unpleasant conversation. "No," he insisted, threading his fingers through Noah's. "You'd never hurt me. I believe in you, Noah, and I love you. Come on. Let's go back to Eden."

Noah looked like he wanted to continue protesting. He opened his mouth, but then closed it again, as if changing his mind. When he spoke, his words startled Logan. "Iberia wants to wage war against Eden. I stole a glimpse at their files when I was on board their ship. They're waiting for us to be weakened by a potential civil war, and then plan to strike."

Logan cursed and picked Noah up hastily. "All the more reason why we should get out of here."

Noah set his head on Logan's shoulder, drained of strength. "I know, Logan," he said. "But... please, don't take me back to Genesis. Please."

Logan knew he should be explaining to Noah the necessity of returning to Eden's capital. There, he could get treatment for his problem, the best of care, and top-notch medical equipment to monitor his condition. But Noah's voice held so much grief and despair that Logan couldn't bear to add to it.

"Okay, baby. We'll go somewhere else. Somewhere just for the two of us."

"That sounds nice." Noah's smile was tired and dazed. "But just as long as I don't hurt you."

"You won't."

Logan entered the hovercraft and secured Noah into a seat, strapping him down with a safety belt. Since he was still aware of the less than perfect state he'd found Noah in, he also brought up the medical sensors embedded in the hovercraft's systems. He held Noah's hand as the equipment performed the scan, and was very relieved when the results proclaimed Noah clear of additional injuries.

He intended to pull away and start the hovercraft for their journey home, but before he could do so, Noah wrapped his arms around his shoulders. "I'm sorry. I'm sorry for everything."

The words were on Logan's lips. He wanted to say "you have nothing to be sorry for." It would even be true, to a certain extent, since these unfortunate circumstances weren't Noah's fault. Noah hadn't asked to be brought into existence, only to be treated as an inferior life-form after that. He had always done his best for Eden, for Logan, and for Uriel. But telling Noah all that would just make light of his regrets and concerns, and Logan didn't have the heart to do it.

He kissed Noah's temple and whispered, "Get some rest. We'll be home soon."

Noah nodded, and his eyes drifted closed. In that moment, Logan wanted nothing more than to hold him and protect him forever. The bitter taste of helplessness filled his mouth, and he forced himself to move away from Noah and slide into the piloting seat.

Logan input the necessary commands and the hovercraft obediently took off, heading back toward Eden. As they left Iberia behind, Logan activated the vidscreen and dialed Uriel's frequency.

Uriel's face popped up on the screen a few moments later. "Well, did you find him?"

"Yeah," Logan replied. "He's exhausted, but otherwise okay. Insofar as he can be at least."

"I'll have Hugh ready a room to tend to his injuries."

Logan shook his head. "We're not coming back to Genesis, Uriel. Noah is afraid to be there."

The long pause that followed made Logan wonder if the vidscreen was broken and Uriel had somehow abandoned the conversation. Finally, Uriel snapped out of his trance. "Fair enough. Privacy might be good for him. Where will you be taking him? Maybe I could provide supplies and send in anything else he might need."

Logan was reluctant to share his secret with anyone, but he couldn't keep it from Uriel, not under these circumstances. "Remember that island, the one they used to call Hawaii?"

"I know of it, yes," Uriel replied. "How can I not?"

"Well, then, you must know that after they made sure the volcanoes were dead, the land that survived the Great Eruption went up for sale. My parents were always a bit eccentric, so they decided to invest."

Many people had deemed it strange. Despite the passage of the years, the area hadn't healed, and the paradise it had once been was gone forever. But his mother had once told Logan that love could bring out good things even from the darkness, and Logan had many beautiful memories from the dark beaches, in a place that had once been torn apart by fire and ash.

"I have a house in the area," he said. "No one really knows about it except Raze, since most of the people who owned property are dead, and the purist regime showed no interest in it. I think Noah will be safe there."

Uriel nodded, and something knowing glittered in his eyes. "Send me the coordinates. It's close enough to Eden that I can fly there myself. I won't share the information with anyone."

"Not even Hugh?"

Uriel rubbed his eyes in an open display of fatigue. "We need Hugh to research a cure for Noah, but he's not liable to get over what I revealed, not so quickly. So I'm keeping a close eye on him, just in case."

Despite himself, Logan felt a pang of concern. Uriel was still Noah's brother and Raze's lover. "Are you going to be okay on your own?"

Uriel smiled, although it didn't reach his eyes. "I'll be fine. Raze will probably be back soon. I hope so, at least."

The yearning in Uriel's gaze was undeniable, but Logan didn't acknowledge it. He could not. In the end, he wasn't the one Uriel needed, and in fact, even if he and Noah did return, they'd only bring an additional burden to Uriel.

"I'll take care of him," he offered, perhaps more clumsily than he'd have liked.

"I know. I trust you."

Logan realized then that in spite of everything, he trusted Uriel as well. He couldn't make sense of his own feelings when it came to Noah's brother, but there *was* a level of trust there, which came with the relief that Noah wouldn't have to worry about him and Uriel arguing.

"I'll be at the house in a few hours," he said. "Be careful, Uriel. Don't take any chances."

Uriel chuckled. "I can watch my own back, Logan. Don't worry about it."

The vidlink went dead, and Logan wished he felt more certain of their future. He realized he hadn't told Uriel about Iberia's plans, but perhaps it was better this way. They could talk about it in person once they all reached the house.

Noah awoke when they were about fifteen minutes away from the islands. He slid out of his seat and walked up to Logan. "Where are we going?"

He sounded more alert, and when Logan stole a look at him, he found none of the pallor and exhaustion he'd seen when they'd left the Beaches of the Dead. "My parents owned a sort of holiday home in the Hawaiian Archipelago. We used to spend summers there, and it's safe and private."

Noah leaned against him, his smile gentle, yet sad. "Sounds nice."

"It was, and I want to share it with you."

He knew taking Noah there would nudge certain wounds open, but at the same time, he wanted Noah to realize once and for all that he had nothing to do with the virus. His own soul and consciousness were separate from Uriel's. Half the time, Logan couldn't understand himself when it came to Uriel, but he did know that he didn't want Noah to carry the burden his brother was already shouldering, whether it was warranted or not.

The group of tiny islands soon came within view, and Logan gestured for Noah to sit down and prepare for their descent. Noah complied, even though he kept shooting curious glances out the window. His sadness seemed to drift away, leaving behind awe and no small amount of eagerness.

Logan could empathize, since he'd once felt the same. The Great Eruption—actually a series of eruptions on five of the largest islands—had destroyed most of the archipelago, but it was still a sight to be seen, in a different way. Despite the roller coaster of emotions roiling in his chest, Logan found himself smiling, because he truly did want to share this with Noah.

He landed the jet on the miniature island that belonged to him, a remnant of the once far larger Kaua'i. The house itself stood a few hundred feet away. It wasn't large, a two story structure that had its own solar-powered generator. Logan had done his best to keep it in a reasonable shape, even when cyborgs had been struggling under the purist regime. He'd had the foresight to bring all the systems and utilities up to date after Uriel had taken over, so he knew they would be comfortable here.

Noah leaped out of the jet before Logan could even help him out. He took off his sandals and walked through the black sand, marveling at its consistency. "This is very strange."

Logan followed Noah's example and joined his lover on the black beach. "It is, isn't it? But it's not a bad strange."

Noah plopped down on the ground, sweeping his fingers through the sand and idly watching it fall back in a strange mimic of an hourglass. "No," he said, "not a bad strange."

Logan sat down next to Noah and discarded his boots. Noah naturally leaned against him, and together they lay on the beach in silence, watching as the sun's rays hit the clear waters.

Logan played with the ends of Noah's hair as his lover set his head on his chest. "It's so peaceful here," he whispered. "I have to wonder how that's even possible."

"One wouldn't think so, right?" Logan smiled knowingly. "No trees, black sand, a place that once witnessed so much destruction. But life is a cycle, Noah. An ending is often a new beginning, and a sign for rebirth."

"Do you think I will be reborn?" Noah asked quietly.

Logan closed his eyes to contain the tears choking him. Yet again, he wanted to say Noah wouldn't have to be reborn, that they'd manage to find a cure for his condition. And maybe that was true. Logan hadn't given up hope—it was far too soon to know. He had to believe Noah could survive this. But Noah didn't believe that, and Logan couldn't force his hopes onto his lover.

So instead he said, "Beautiful things are always reborn. And I'll wait for you. Always."

Noah cried softly against Logan's chest, and his tears burned Logan. Hot and wet, they seemed to scorch straight through his skin and touch his soul. Silence fell, broken only by Noah's soft sobs, and Logan held Noah close, wishing he'd never have to let go.

Uriel arrived about one hour after the two of them, alone like he had promised. As soon as he saw his brother, Noah bounded toward him. Uriel enveloped him in a fierce embrace, and as Logan watched them, he idly thought they looked like they'd been separated for years, not mere hours.

Logan left them to their reunion, granting them privacy as he retreated into the house. He had decided that from now on, he would respect Uriel's bond with Noah, and that included giving the two of them some space. His idea kind of backfired on him when Noah tracked him down a few minutes later. Logan took one look at Noah's unhappy scowl and his hackles rose. "What is it?" he asked, meeting Noah halfway and embracing him tightly. "What's wrong?"

It was a stupid question since there were so many wrong things in their lives right now Logan didn't even want to think about it. But Noah knew Logan was referring to this particular situation. He sighed as he melted into Logan's embrace. "You didn't greet Uriel."

"Oh." Logan kicked himself for that. "I thought the two of you wished to talk alone. I didn't want to be in the way."

"You're never in the way," Uriel said from the doorway. "I appreciate the courtesy, but really, it's not necessary. I have no doubt Noah shares everything with you."

Noah nodded against Logan's chest, and Logan was torn between confusion, gratitude, and affection. In the end, he pushed those emotions aside for the benefit of practicalities. "You said you'd be bringing supplies?" he asked Uriel.

Together, the three of them made their way to the hovercraft Uriel had flown in. Uriel had indeed brought them many things they would need for their stay, from clothing and foodstuffs to medical equipment. It took hours to install everything inside the house, but they worked side by side companionably, and for a while, Logan could pretend today didn't rank high up among the worst days of his life. Noah obediently allowed Uriel to check him over again, and Uriel decreed him to have survived his little adventure free of any injuries.

By the time they finished everything, the sun had already set, and they sat on the dark beach, watching moonlight dance over the waves. Logan would have liked to cling to the peacefulness of the moment, but he hadn't forgotten what Noah had told him. "Iberia is planning a war against Eden," he told Uriel.

"You heard that on board their ship?" Uriel inquired.

Naturally, the words weren't addressed to Logan, but to Noah. "Yes," Noah told his brother. "For the moment, they're wary of our forces, but if we falter or succumb to civil war, they'll attack."

Uriel stared out into the distance, silent. "You don't seem surprised," Logan commented.

"I expected it," Uriel replied. "Iberia has been rehashing their accords with Germania and Gallia. Eden doesn't have a lot of friends in that part of the world. The previous Council didn't think we would need them."

"It's not your fault, Uriel," Noah said. "Whatever happens, it's not your fault."

Uriel's lips twisted into a small parody of a smile, but he didn't go against his brother's opinion. "We won't let it get to that. Eden is still stronger than they think."

Logan wanted to believe that, but there were too many factors involved, too many things that could go wrong, and too many conflicting agendas for him to have any certainties. From its beginnings twenty years back, Eden had only ever been as strong as the Guiding Light, and people were not ready for the sudden shift. Politicians like Abraham Zion resented the change and suspected foul play when it came to deaths of the previous Council members, and in that regard, they weren't even completely wrong. The irony in all this was that he found he didn't care, or he cared very little. Somewhere along the line, Noah had become his world, and whether or not Eden was involved in a war was secondary to Noah's situation.

He pulled Noah into his lap and buried his face in Noah's hair. His lover came willingly and settled down in his embrace, curling against him like a contented cat. A few minutes later, Logan realized Noah had fallen asleep.

He hadn't expected that, but he supposed it made sense. Doing his best not to wake Noah, Logan got up and headed back toward the house. Uriel followed, a silent, thoughtful shadow.

Logan set Noah down on the bed in what had once been his parents' room and covered him with a thick quilt. In his sleep, Noah looked peaceful, blond curls framing his cheeks, chest rising steadily. He looked like an angel, and Logan refrained from kissing him only because he didn't want to disturb his slumber.

He realized Uriel wasn't in the room when he turned away from Noah. Logan stepped out of the bedroom and found Uriel waiting for him in the lounge, seated on the low couch. "Anything from Hugh?" Logan asked as he joined the other man.

Uriel grimaced. "For the moment, the best thing we can do is to provide physical and emotional stability for Noah. It was a good idea to bring him here, since it will lessen his anxiety. His memories of Genesis and the duties he'd assign to himself there would just make his condition worse." He paused and stared at his hands, as if bracing himself for the following words. "Hugh is considering a stabilizer agent made out of my blood, but we don't know if that will work. And even if it does, it would be only temporary."

"I'm sure there has to be some solution," Logan said, more for his own benefit than for Uriel's.

Uriel looked up at him and shot him a tired smile. "Yes, of course. We'll find a way. We're more advanced now than we used to be when cloning was first discovered and banned. Besides, Noah is special. We won't give up."

Out of the blue, Uriel hugged him. Logan was so surprised that he didn't even know where to put his hands or how to touch Uriel. It didn't help that, in some ways, Uriel's body felt just like Noah's, his hair soft against Logan's cheek, the press of his slender form familiar and maybe even a little welcome.

It wasn't arousal that gripped him, though, but protectiveness, a protectiveness very similar to the one that had once caused him to reach out to a lost young man who considered himself a copy of someone better. Uriel wasn't Noah, but in other ways, he was vulnerable.

So in spite of everything, Logan hugged Uriel back. When Uriel broke away, he whispered, "Keep him safe, Logan. You can do more than I ever could."

There was nothing that needed to be said beyond that. They understood each other, and perhaps even had a friendship of sorts, one based on loving Noah and Raze, albeit in different ways. Logan led Uriel out of the house and to his hovercraft without a word, and Uriel didn't say anything either as he boarded the aircraft.

The hovercraft took off, and then disappeared into the distance. When Logan's enhanced eyesight lost track of the ship, he returned to the house and slid back into the bedroom. Careful not to wake Noah, he curled around his lover and closed his eyes. He didn't remember falling asleep.

Chapter Five

A FEW days passed as Noah got accustomed to living in the little house with Logan. Things didn't change, and yet, they were so different. Logan held him, kissed him, hugged him, but never once did he try to make love with him again.

Noah had moments during which he wondered if that had been a one-time thing, maybe born more out of pity than actual lust.

And then he saw it. At first, he thought he was imagining things, since his hair was naturally very blond, and the difference didn't stand out. But he was realistic enough not to hide from the truth. The morning of their third day there, he locked himself inside the bathroom and stared at the streaks of white in his hair.

He wanted to cry, especially since he knew this was just the first sign of worse things to come. He wondered if Logan had noticed, if he'd kept it from Noah to be kind and not point out the obvious, the truth they'd been dancing around even when they tried to force themselves to face it.

A knock sounded at the door, followed by Logan's voice, heavy with concern. "Noah? Are you all right?"

Noah stared at himself in the mirror. He didn't look much different, but at this rate, there was no telling how long his beauty would last. So when he opened the door, he smiled invitingly at Logan. "I'm fine," he said, leaning against Logan's chest. "Don't worry so much."

"How can I not…. Noah, what are you doing?"

Noah continued to nuzzle Logan's neck, worming his hand between their bodies, reaching for Logan's dick. Inside, he was panicking, because he didn't know what he'd do if Logan rejected him. "Isn't it obvious?"

He tried to sound coy, seductive, but his voice came out too desperate to be sensual. Logan gripped his wrist and kept him from going further. "Baby, no. This isn't a good idea."

Noah didn't try to push his lover. He slumped against Logan's chest, suddenly feeling drained of strength. He said nothing as Logan picked him up in his arms, then carried him to the couch.

They ended up huddled together on the comfortable settee. At one point, Logan reached for Noah's hair, and Noah realized his lover was curling his fingers around the white strands he'd discovered minutes earlier. So Noah had been right. His lover had seen them.

"This is happening," he said with a quiet sigh. "We can't ignore it."

"No, we can't," Logan replied, "but we also don't have to believe there is no solution to it."

"Maybe there is, maybe there isn't," Noah answered, clutching Logan's vest convulsively. "I don't know what I'm doing, Logan. I want to spend the last days of my life with you, to feel you touch me before I decompose into something that barely resembles me anymore. And then I remember that I'm afraid, that I could hurt you, and I want to scream, and I'm so scared…."

He realized he was rambling, crying, and shaking, but he couldn't stop himself even when he knew he should, even when he was aware his words hurt Logan. The confessions tumbled out of him like a stream he couldn't stop, and he was rocking against Logan, needing him, wanting him, afraid for him, wishing he could have deserved him.

Logan flipped him on his back on the couch, and when Logan's weight landed on top of him, Noah felt some of the tension inside him drain out. His tears dried, and he inhaled deeply, struggling for calm, or rather, looking for it in Logan's steady gaze.

"I'm here, Noah," Logan whispered. "I'm not going anywhere. But I'm scared, too. Not because I think you might hurt me, but…. You left when we first made love. I can't imagine… I don't want to lose you. In any way."

Noah realized he'd made a mistake in fleeing, but he didn't want to blame that rashness on the beautiful moments they had shared. And then there was his confusion over the effects of his bioenergy on Logan. It hadn't hurt him, and Noah knew it had been quite out of control the one time they'd had sex.

Where did that leave them? He had no idea, and he felt so completely lost. He wanted to bury himself under Logan's skin, in Logan's heart, and forget he even existed as a separate entity.

"Close your eyes," Logan said from above him. He was so close now that Noah couldn't quite focus his gaze on him, so he eagerly complied, directing the rest of his senses to concentrate on Logan. He could easily get drunk on Logan's scent alone, and he wouldn't have minded if they just lay there like that together for the rest of the day.

But then Logan's sure hands trailed over his sides and slid under his clothes. Noah couldn't help a small gasp, and Logan shushed him. "Relax. I'll take care of you."

With almost excruciating gentleness, Logan took off Noah's garments. Noah tried to help, and he tried to respond in turn, but Logan held him back, not allowing him to do much. Maybe Noah should have protested, but he really couldn't bring himself to, not when Logan had him naked far sooner than Noah had expected. Logan's hands were warm on his skin, strong and slightly callused, and Noah couldn't remember why he'd ever been wary or afraid, or how he'd managed to summon any other emotion than affection and arousal.

Truth be told, there was no separating the two, not in this. Logan's touches were sensual, yes, but they also held a degree of kindness that reached out to Noah's very soul. No, not kindness— this went far beyond that. It was almost worshipful, but not in that distant yet invasive way the Guiding Light had been touched. Logan kept brushing tender kisses all over his face while his fingers explored every inch of Noah's torso. Noah moaned, and he must have said something, although he wasn't sure exactly what, because Logan went on to whisper, "It's all right. Be patient. I'll give you everything you need."

Noah believed him, because this was Logan, and Logan had somehow managed to become the most important person in Noah's life. And Logan knew what Noah needed, perhaps better than Noah himself. He progressed down Noah's body, his fingers zeroing in on Noah's nipples, rubbing lightly, just enough to make a zing of sensation course through him. Noah's cock, already hard from Logan's proximity and touch, throbbed painfully, but in a paradoxical twist, Noah didn't want to rush things along. He wanted this slow sway of emotion, the barely there touches, and the gentle caresses. It was far more meaningful than what Noah had reached for in his shock-fueled despair. When Logan held him, he felt alive, like nothing could ever hurt him. He felt loved, and that was his clearest, most beautiful truth.

Logan did indeed keep his promise and gave Noah what he wanted. He lightly sucked Noah's nipples, triggering tiny explosions through him. As he teased the tender buds, he reached between their bodies and slowly massaged Noah's cock.

The feel of Logan's palm on his dick might have made Noah come on the spot, but Logan's caresses were winding a lazy spell of seduction around him. His body floated in a mix of lust and relaxation, and he didn't want it to end, not yet, not ever. Yes, the pleasure level increased with every second that passed, but Logan was the one who built it up, tenderly, gradually, yet with a degree of passion that couldn't be denied.

He kissed down Noah's abdomen even as he massaged Noah's testes. When he at last took Noah's cock in his mouth, Noah was flying, free in his desire for Logan.

A few sucks of Logan's talented mouth, and Noah found his peak. He'd have been embarrassed at how quickly he came, but he couldn't bring himself to feel shame. He could only cling to this moment, to this happiness, and see past the pleasure Logan had given him into the emotions that had brought it about.

Noah floated out of his trance solely because he was well aware he had not done anything to reciprocate. He opened his eyes and pushed Logan back on the couch. His lover resisted for about half a second before gripping Noah's hand and guiding it to his cock.

Logan hadn't taken his clothes off. He'd only undone his pants enough to give Noah access to his shaft. Noah would have liked to do more, to give Logan the same ecstasy he'd received. But Logan held him tightly as Noah jacked him off, and in that embrace, Noah read the same feelings that had tumbled him over the edge. Noah loved him so much he couldn't even breathe. Sparks erupted over his fingertips, and Logan's body went rigid. Noah would have been worried he'd hurt his lover, but Logan buried his face in Noah's hair as he came. And then they just sat there, holding on to each other, breathing hard, both of them trembling with the aftermath of their climaxes and enjoying the sizzling electricity between them.

Logan was the one who moved first, which didn't surprise Noah, since he didn't want to move—ever. "I'll be right back," Logan whispered against Noah's lips.

Noah couldn't resist stealing a brief kiss and noted with delight that Logan tasted like him. Logan lingered in the lip-lock, twining their tongues together, taking possession of Noah's mouth. When he pulled away, he did so with a disgruntled groan. "You tempt me too much."

Noah couldn't really feel guilty about that, but he respected Logan's desires and he let his lover go. He lay back down on the couch, idly sucking his fingers clean of Logan's spunk. Logan tasted salty with a slight tinge of something that was purely him. He wondered if he could get Logan to take him once they recovered a bit. He hoped so.

Logan returned a little while later, carrying one of the medical items Uriel had left behind—a container that held a vial meant to draw blood. As Logan sat down again, Noah couldn't help but ask, "What are you doing?"

The answer was pretty obvious, since Logan gently gripped Noah's arm and pressed the vial to his skin. "Blood sample. We need answers, and hopefully this will help." He finished filling the vial of blood and set it away in the receptacle.

Noah bit his lip, something cold pooling in his stomach. Had Logan only touched him so he could get the blood sample? Had the gentleness, the affection been a lie? Not that he could expect more. Logan was probably trying to help, and he'd given Noah more than he ever deserved. For a little while, he'd been more than a clone, but that didn't change the truth, no matter what he'd been trying to tell himself.

Logan gripped his chin, keeping him from pulling away. "Look at me," he said earnestly. "Look at me."

Noah did, and when he saw Logan through a film of tears, he angrily wiped his eyes. Logan sighed. "I'm so sorry, Noah. I know this isn't very romantic, but it's necessary. I want to hold you in my arms every night and kiss you every single day, but we can't do that unless we're sure it's safe." He pulled Noah into his arms, the hold as fierce as it had been gentle. "I need you so much."

Just like that, Noah's feelings of self-loathing dissipated. He'd been cruel not to think of how hard this must be for Logan, cruel to make demands when the situation strained Logan so much. He would have berated himself for it more, but this wasn't something he could help. And Noah wanted to live, not so much for himself, but for Logan, for what they had together.

He couldn't say any of this, so he relaxed in Logan's arms and nodded. Slowly, his lover's familiar heat drained his tension, leaving behind only exhaustion. When he drifted off to sleep, he did so with the knowledge that he was safe.

LOGAN HATED hurting Noah. Even if drawing blood had been for a good cause, he still ached when he remembered the crushed look in Noah's eyes. Gently, he petted Noah's hair, feeling more helpless than ever.

Truth be told, he was very much aware of what the passage of time meant for Noah. He'd noticed the graying hair, although he hadn't wanted to point it out to his lover. Being here seemed to help

Noah's morale, but the sexual relationship between them also made Logan's fears resurface every time.

Noah needed physical affection, and denying him made things worse. His emotional instability was a fact, but Logan wasn't quite sure as to how sex between them affected Noah at a cellular level.

With a sigh, Logan got up, still holding his lover. Noah didn't stir as Logan carried him to the bedroom. He grumbled slightly when Logan sat him on the bed, whispering Logan's name under his breath. Logan's heart clenched, and not for the first time in the past few days, he wondered how someone so beautiful could be in so much danger.

He tucked Noah in and left the room out of the sheer fear that he'd succumb to his desire to crawl next to Noah in bed. It wasn't that he wouldn't have liked to do so, but he expected Uriel to fly in any moment now, and he wanted to talk to the man before Noah woke up.

He'd have liked to test the blood sample he'd gotten, but he was no doctor. While he knew how to work scanners and a lot of medical equipment, he didn't want to take any chances when it came to Noah. He'd looked at Noah's DNA before, but he hadn't noticed the cellular degeneration. Uriel had told him Logan couldn't have spotted the disease before it had fully manifested, but to a certain extent, he still felt he was to blame for not seeing this sooner.

Fortunately, Uriel arrived fifteen minutes later. He looked tired, dark circles underneath his eyes. Raze wrapped a protective arm around him as they descended from the jet.

Logan hadn't seen his friend since the day he'd learned about Noah's condition. Uriel had told him Raze had returned to Genesis, but he'd been sketchy on the details, perhaps because Noah had been around to hear their conversations.

Raze released Uriel and hugged Logan tightly. "I heard," he whispered in Logan's ear. "I'm so sorry."

"Not your fault," Logan replied.

"Should have been there for you."

Logan broke their embrace and arched a brow at his old friend. "Why do I have the feeling there's more going on than Uriel's told me?"

71

Uriel shot him a weak smile. "All things considered, that part was pretty obvious. Where's Noah?"

"Inside. Sleeping."

Something in his tone must have alarmed Uriel, because he scowled. "Is everything all right?"

"Nothing is all right, but you already know that."

He tried to keep his tone from being biting, and in the end, it came out disheartened. When his friends didn't say anything, Logan guided them away from the plane. They sat together on the beach, and Logan recounted a brief summary of what had been going on for the past few days. It was a little awkward to explain his sexual life to his lover's brother, but he made do, and Uriel was strikingly understanding.

"Sexual contact is comforting and healthy in a regular situation," he said. "The endorphins that flood the bloodstream should benefit Noah. But... we're not exactly normal."

"You've given thought to this," Logan guessed.

Uriel nodded. "Some, yes. The blood sample you took would help clarify my suspicions." He rubbed his eyes tiredly. "Noah needs you, and I know this is hard, but until I have some results, it might be best for you to abstain."

Logan had expected that. "I don't suppose you have any good news."

"Actually, Hugh managed to create a serum," Raze answered, "the one Uriel was telling you about. It should help stabilize Noah's condition. We have the first batch in the jet. We'll stay here while you administer it, just to make sure there aren't any side effects, but we've tested it heavily in the lab and it should be fine."

Uncertainty and fear swelled inside Logan. Experimental drugs could harm Noah, and the "should" was no guarantee. But he had to trust that Uriel knew what he was doing, so he nodded. "Good idea."

To distract himself from his confusing emotions, he brought up the other issues that had been on his mind. "What of the situation with Abraham Zion? Iberia?"

Raze and Uriel shared a look that Logan didn't like at all. "What is it?" he prodded. "You can tell me, Raze. You know you can."

"You don't need extra concerns added to Noah's problems," Raze argued.

No, Logan didn't, but he also had to know. Uncertainty was far worse. At least having the knowledge would help him make the right decision should he ever have to protect Noah from an outside threat.

Uriel must have guessed his resolve, because he proceeded to explain, "It's getting worse. Raze temporarily managed to settle tensions in Zion, but it didn't last. I've been traveling throughout Eden to help other cyborgs regain the use of their implants. We're going to need the military force if Iberia attacks. But seeing my focus on cyborg citizens makes the purist part of our society nervous. Voices argue that we're building up to a cyborg militaristic state."

Logan cursed under his breath. "And by voices you mean Abraham Zion."

"Among others, yes. We have given him a warning to cease these encouragements to revolt, but there's only so much we can do while he doesn't attack anyone. At this rate, I'm not sure whether we'll be strong enough to withstand an assault from an outside force."

"I've taken a stealth force to Germania to look into the alliance," Raze continued. "They are still afraid of us, and they want what we have to offer, so they're not about to jump into war just like that. Still, I'm very unsettled."

That was saying something, because Raze never got unsettled without good reason. Knowing Raze, he'd probably been in and out of Eden on a daily basis, which was likely one of the reasons he hadn't contacted Logan until now. "What explanation did you come up with for my absence?" he asked.

Uriel shrugged. "That was easy. No one seemed surprised when we said Noah was sick. I suppose a lot of people expected it to happen." He let out a short, bitter laugh. "If there's anything good about this whole debacle, it's that Noah is at least away from Genesis and not considered dangerous by our enemies."

Uriel was right. Most people, Edenians and those from other countries, would assume there was no point to focusing on the Guiding Light's clone, who would eventually die anyway. While Logan refused to accept that conclusion, the fact that it existed in the minds of others could actually help.

They didn't get the chance to talk more about the political situation in Eden. Noah walked out of the house, and even from the distance, Logan noticed his tense posture. A wave from Uriel had Noah relaxing and padding to their side.

"Hi," he said, greeting his brother. "You're early."

Uriel smiled as he got up and hugged Noah. From his place, Logan could see Uriel's pained expression. He wasn't early. Noah had forgotten when Uriel was supposed to arrive.

Logan almost said it too, but he stopped himself just in time. Some things often seemed to slip Noah's mind these days, like losing track of a thought rather than forgetting specific issues. This was the first major thing he'd failed to remember, and it jarred Logan, more so since it came so soon after they'd made love.

"I brought you something," Uriel said when they broke apart. "A serum that should help."

Noah perked up visibly. "It will heal me?"

The breathless tone held so much hope it nearly crushed Logan inside. He shot to his feet and hugged Noah with perhaps more enthusiasm than he'd have liked. Uriel obviously didn't have the heart to explain, and neither did Logan, so Raze was the one who spoke. "It's more of a temporary cure, but we're still working on something permanent."

Logan felt the tremor in Noah's body, but when he spoke, his lover's voice was steady. "I see. You have no idea how grateful I am."

Raze and Logan carried the boxes of serum into the impromptu medical bay Logan had set up for Noah. Once everything was in place, Noah sat down on a bench and offered his arm. "Time to see how it works."

Logan picked up one of the vials of serum, but his hands were trembling so badly he couldn't administer it. Raze took over so smoothly nothing seemed wrong. Logan and Uriel framed Noah, and if Noah noticed their nervousness, he made no note of it.

Raze slowly injected the serum, and for a few moments, they waited, all of them breathless with a mix of fear and anticipation. Logan tried not to be too obvious about it, but he suspected he failed abysmally. When Noah gasped, Logan's composure snapped. "Baby? What is it? Are you in pain?"

Noah shook his head and crawled into his lap. His body vibrated with barely restrained energy, and despite Noah's wordless assurance, Logan's concern skyrocketed. He half-expected electricity to burst from his lover, as it regularly did in moments of emotional intensity. It didn't happen. Instead, Noah slumped in Logan's arms, panting, but otherwise seeming unharmed.

"Baby?" Logan asked again.

"I'm fine, Logan." Noah broke away from him long enough to shoot him a tired smile. "I'm really all right."

Logan believed him, because the lock of gray hair that had triggered Noah's nervous breakdown had disappeared. Until now, Logan hadn't even realized how drained and unsettled Noah had been—or hadn't wanted to see it. There was clarity and purpose in him again, and his vulnerability mingled with the same undeniable strength that made Logan fall in love with him over and over again.

"It worked," he said with a grin. "It worked, Noah."

Noah nodded and melted against him for a second time. Logan would have felt ecstatic about it, but over Noah's head, he met Uriel's eyes. The despair he saw in them made his blood turn to ice, and he hugged Noah tighter. Hiding the fear inside his heart, he added, "We'll be all right."

Now if only he could make himself believe it.

Chapter Six

THE SERUM gave Noah renewed hope, and for the first time in what seemed like forever, he felt like he might have a chance at happiness. Even if Uriel had warned him it was a temporary cure, Noah believed in his brother and had faith that eventually they'd find something more permanent.

His bout of optimism didn't last. The day after the visit, Uriel contacted them with the blood test results. From the moment he saw Uriel's face, Noah knew the answers to Logan's questions wouldn't be good. He wanted to run away and curl under the covers in the bedroom they shared, but instead, he stood his ground in front of the communications console. "Well?"

"The blood sample showed that sexual arousal does indeed affect you. It's not a... direct thing, not as you might think. It's connected to our specific nature. You might have noticed that pleasure often causes our bioenergy to emerge."

It was a little embarrassing to discuss something like this with his brother, but shyness would have been idiotic. "Yes, but insofar as I can tell, it doesn't hurt Logan."

"Of course it doesn't," Uriel replied. "This energy is targeted, and very different from other ways we use our power. But Logan isn't the concern here. It's you. The pulsations of power are unstable. They can help you, but they can also harm you and trigger a further deterioration in your cell structure."

Noah remembered his trip to Iberia. He'd used a ridiculous amount of bioenergy, far more than would have been wise, which had caused him to faint on the beach. His emotional ups and downs couldn't be denied. Had his flight worsened his condition? The thought was staggering.

Logan wrapped an arm around his waist, holding him up when he might have collapsed. "What exactly are you saying? Do you have any advice?"

"I wish I had all the answers," Uriel said tiredly. "I don't. According to Hugh, it would be best not to take any chances and stick to platonic relations. I know it won't be easy, but beyond that...."

Noah understood. He hated that he couldn't be with Logan sexually, but their intimacy went beyond the carnal level. "Thank you for telling us, Uriel. And thank you for all your help. I... I wish I could be there for you."

He wasn't an idiot. Even if Logan had tried to hide the truth from him, Noah could tell the situation in Genesis was worsening. Noah would always carry the burden of having made it worse, and he'd always wonder what would have happened if he hadn't killed the previous Council members. But it was too late for regrets now. He needed to get better so he could be with Logan and help Uriel.

His words drew a small smile from his brother. "I miss you, Noah, but I'm happiest knowing you're safe. We'll keep in touch, all right? I'll drop by as often as I can. Logan, take care of him for me."

Logan nodded. "Will do. And you take care of Raze." The vidscreen went black, and Logan guided Noah away from the console.

Days passed. Noah and Logan spent a lot of time on the beach, swimming, talking, reminiscing. They kissed and touched, but they never went too far with their caresses. It was frustrating, but Noah felt lucky he had this. In every gentle kiss, he felt Logan's love for him, and that was more precious than anything.

As promised, Uriel visited, and sometimes Raze came with him. They brought more of the stabilizing serum. Noah noted with concern that Uriel looked worse and worse. And then the day came when the plane didn't carry Uriel at all, only Raze, and Noah panicked. "Is he all right? What's going on?"

"He's fine," Raze replied automatically. His bland words wouldn't have convinced a child, let alone Noah, and Raze must have realized it. "Okay, he's not fine. He's very tired. The war effort is taking a toll on him, and he's not sleeping well. I left him in Julian's care, so that he could try to get some rest."

"He's healing more cyborgs, I take it." Noah bit his lip so hard it bled. "I should have helped. I should have supported him."

"It's not your fault, Noah," Raze told him, but he sounded so exhausted and heartbroken that Noah didn't believe him.

The next day, Noah awoke as usual in Logan's arms, but when he went to the bathroom, he almost screamed. Overnight, lines had appeared on his previously youthful face, and three quarters of his hair had gone white. Some of it was falling out, and Noah spent ten minutes hyperventilating over what to do before he gripped the scissors, deciding to shear it all off.

Logan arrived before Noah could do anything stupid. He helped cut Noah's hair to a more manageable length, whispering soft words of comfort as he worked. As the long locks fell to the floor, Noah felt more aware than ever of what he was losing. He didn't have the strength to answer Logan, or even to look at him.

But his lover was nothing if not persistent. He swiftly completed his task, and then took him to their medical bay. They contacted Raze, who directed them to Hugh Wells. "Double the serum dose," the doctor advised them, "and please, try to remain calm. Emotional distress will worsen your condition."

The stabilizing substance worked this time around too, but it became less potent day by day. Two weeks after Logan had first started to administer it, Noah lay in bed, watching his skin peel off with a sort of sick fascination. It almost looked harmless, like he'd been in the sun too long. But Noah knew better, knew the real reason behind it. He felt it, beyond what he saw in the mirror, deep inside. It wasn't a particular type of discomfort. If that had been the case, he could have countered it somehow. He just ached.

Logan caressed his now-short hair gently, and Noah had a disheartened moment during which he wished Logan had never fallen in love with him. Clearly, the serum wouldn't prolong his life for much longer, and it was always the ones left behind who suffered most.

"Hey," Logan whispered, "I know you're feeling a bit out of it, but you need to eat. I made you a light snack. Do you think you can stomach at least some of it?"

Noah blinked and realized that indeed, Logan had brought him some food. It was nothing complicated, just a salad, since these days Noah couldn't digest much else. Nausea still roiled through Noah, but he forced himself to comply.

He chewed steadily, even if he almost gagged at the taste. Intellectually he knew the fresh fruit was a delicacy, supplied by Uriel and Raze specifically for his needs, but his body insisted on protesting. He only managed a few bites before he stopped, breathing like he'd run a marathon. Logan took the plate and set it away without comment. He offered Noah a sip of water, and Noah drank steadily.

"Can I ask you a question?" he inquired as he lay back down.

"Anything," Logan replied, kissing his temple.

"If you hadn't been here with me, where would you be?"

He already knew the answer, but he wanted to hear it anyway. "With Raze," Logan said without a moment of hesitation. "Helping him in Genesis."

"Do you regret it, not doing that?"

Logan shook his head. "Raze has been my friend since we were kids. He's practically a brother to me. But I've never loved anyone like I do you. I'll never regret anything I do for you."

If Noah had felt particularly selfless, he'd have told Logan to leave. It was unlikely his lover would have agreed, but Noah might have tried. But in a way, he was relieved Logan wasn't in Genesis. At least here, Logan wouldn't be exposed to whatever horrors the purist adepts managed to cook up. Maybe it was cruel of him. Maybe Logan's absence made things even harder for Raze and Uriel, and staying here to care for Noah was harder for Logan than anything the purists could think of. Nonetheless, he didn't run the chance of mortal peril, and that was at least one good thing about the situation—perhaps the only good thing.

As he thought this, a wave of pain rushed over him. Noah went rigid and released a choked cry. The world went hazy around the edges. He heard Logan calling out his name, but his lover's voice reached him through a veil, so distant it scared him. Noah tried to focus on it regardless, but his efforts proved futile. The fog just got worse, and Noah flailed, trying to get a grip, desperate to cling to Logan. He'd thought he'd gotten used to the idea of dying, but he wasn't ready, not nearly ready.

He felt a dull pain in his arm, and then the fog cleared, and he could hear again. "Stay with me, Noah. That's it, baby. Stay with me."

"Logan," Noah heard himself whisper, "I'm scared."

"I know. I know, baby. Don't worry. I'm here. I won't let anything happen to you."

The heat of the beach struck Noah hard, and he hid his face in Logan's chest. He realized that Logan must be carrying him to safety, perhaps in an attempt to find a solution to his predicament. He didn't know if his lover would succeed, but every instinct screamed that he had to stay with Logan, to be with him. He'd have been relieved when the scorching rays faded if Logan's heat hadn't disappeared with them too.

Noah whined, and Logan's hands returned, cupping his cheek. "It's okay, baby. Not going anywhere. Give me a moment."

The moment Logan asked for seemed to take forever. Noah's world began to shake and only steadied when Logan returned to his side. "Hang in there, baby. Just a little while longer."

Noah listened to Logan's voice and it helped him remain cognizant. He lost track of time, Logan's presence his sole anchor. When Logan left again, he almost spiraled into fear and despair, but again, it didn't last long, and then they were moving again.

Voices sounded around them, and Noah experienced a moment of panic during which he wondered if he was hearing things. Or had intruders invaded their little oasis of privacy? The thought made him ache even more.

He realized the truth when a familiar voice reached his ears. "Noah? Can you hear me? Oh no, this isn't happening."

Logan must have brought them back to Genesis. Noah opened his mouth, trying to come up with something to say, to soothe his brother. His vocal cords refused to work, and Noah had never felt more helpless in his life.

Soon they stopped again, and Logan placed Noah on some sort of flat, soft surface. "The serum isn't enough," he heard someone say. The doctor? Hugh? Yes, that was his name. "I had hoped it would buy me more time, but his body is deteriorating faster than expected."

"There has to be something you can do." Logan sounded desperate.

The doctor didn't reply. Noah felt the same slight pain of the puncture, and wasn't it telling that he felt the injections at all? Normally he shouldn't have, but his body had decided to rebel against all modern tech. Still, the medicine helped, and the strange agony disappeared. He blinked and focused on Hugh Wells, who was tending to his wound. "I gave you a shot of a more concentrated serum," the doctor explained. "It should stabilize you for now."

Noah nodded, still a little dizzy. "Thank you," he whispered. "I think it worked." Was that his voice? He sounded hoarse, like he'd been eating sandpaper, or perhaps screaming.

Logan knelt next to him and brushed his lips over his forehead. "Welcome back. Sorry I had to bring you to Genesis. I didn't think I had the skill to handle the situation."

He was still pale, his eyes haunted, and Noah hated himself for bringing Logan such pain. He took a deep breath, remembering the doctor had said emotional distress made things worse. "You did the right thing. I kind of expected it would happen."

And he had. It had been selfish of him to make more demands, although he couldn't honestly say he regretted it. He treasured the time he'd spent with Logan too much.

Uriel and Raze manifested by his side, and Uriel kissed his cheek. He was trembling slightly, and he looked as bad as Noah felt. "You're not taking care of yourself," Noah chastised him.

Uriel released a small chuckle. "Yes, well…. Things haven't exactly been going according to plan. But you're here now. You'll take care of me."

It was a teasing comment—hell, Noah couldn't even take care of himself, let alone Uriel—but that didn't mean he wouldn't have liked to do it. "It hasn't been very fun around here, huh?"

"No, not at all," Hugh replied in Uriel's stead. "Like we originally stated, Noah, you were better off away throughout these past weeks." He paused, as if uncertain. "But things are different now."

"Different how?" Noah asked, already dreading the answer.

Hugh eyed him warily. "Do you think you're ready to hear this?"

"As ready as I'll ever be."

Hugh released a heavy sigh. "Very well. Noah, your condition is worsening too quickly. I don't have the time or the resources to find a cure. I've been trying, believe me, but it would take me years to figure out an actual solution. Your brother has done his best, but we're stretched thin in terms of manpower, and the nature of your DNA makes it impossible for us to divide the project between too many people anyway."

"What exactly are you saying, Hugh?" Logan asked, tightening his hold on Noah.

"At this point, I have one recommendation. I believe that you should consider cryo freeze."

Noah went rigid. It was only because of Logan's embrace that he didn't faint outright. All he could think about was the containers used for cryogenics, trapping him, turning him into a helpless thing.

Suddenly, he couldn't breathe anymore. The nightmares returned, and he felt water invade his lungs. But Logan was there, caressing him, kissing him, holding him close, and he forced himself to the surface.

Containers. Just like the one he'd been created in. A clone, a copy, a tool to be used by people who didn't care. He realized he'd been crying and wiped his eyes. The tears kept coming, and he felt hot and sweaty. No. He refused to lose the battle like this. He was afraid, yes, but for Logan, he'd do it.

With that thought came resolve, and his tears dried. "Is there no other way?" he asked the doctor.

"I'm sorry," Hugh replied, sounding shaken. "I would keep trying, but the procedure needs to happen while you're still stable enough to withstand it."

"And is it safe now?" Logan inquired.

"In my assessment, yes, but I'll do some more tests to be make sure. After this unexpected seizure, we need to ascertain Noah's current condition."

"And if it doesn't work...." Noah trailed off, unable to finish the sentence.

Hugh's expression was glum. "I'll keep trying, but the chances of me finding a cure in the time I'd have at my disposal are slim."

There was no other choice. He had to brave the cryo containers. Truth be told, under different circumstances, he'd have preferred dying over reliving his worst nightmare. But he had Logan, and he owed it to Logan to do everything in his power to live, no matter how much it hurt.

"Okay. Do the tests. We'll go through with the cryo freeze if I'm able to."

As Hugh drew another blood sample, Noah took Logan's hand and squeezed it, trying to give his lover comfort. Logan squeezed his in turn. "This won't hurt him, will it?"

"Not at all," Hugh replied. "I wouldn't go through with it if there were any chance that it might. Cryo freeze is a well-established procedure, Logan. You know that."

It was true. Noah hadn't actually seen a cryo freeze machine in his life, but that was only because of his—or rather, Uriel's—purist upbringing. Prior to the so-called virus, cryogenics had been an increasingly developing field. Research in the area had stopped with Project Uriel, but apparently, Hugh Wells had resurrected it.

Uriel must have known about it too, because he faced Logan. "I've looked over everything. There is no incompatibility between the cryo machine and our DNA. Our bioenergy is triggered by either emotion or will, so it will not emerge while Noah is inside. And even if it did, Noah would not be harmed."

"You've given this a lot of thought," Noah whispered.

"Doctor Wells came to me and explained the situation." His brother smiled, perhaps trying to comfort Noah. It didn't really help. "As soon as I learned of his opinion, I started making arrangements."

If Noah hadn't already been convinced this was the right thing to do, that would have settled it. His brother would never push him into something so difficult if there had been any other way. Even if Noah hadn't admitted the reasons behind his nightmares, Uriel knew him well enough to guess, and he hadn't given Noah the option to back out. It existed, of course it existed, but Uriel didn't see it as a valid choice. In Uriel's mind, refusal meant Noah would die.

Noah couldn't help it. He hugged his brother tightly, wishing he had real words to express everything Uriel meant to him. It occurred to him that if he'd had to come into being as someone's clone, he was happy Uriel was that someone.

As he held on to Uriel, he noticed the doctor had already taken the blood sample to a scanner. Noah broke away from his brother, watching Hugh's motions, his heart hammering. Everyone was silent, well aware that this moment might make the difference between Noah's life and his death.

Finally, Hugh turned away from the scanner. "Well, it seems your cells are still stable enough to go through with the process, but I recommend you do so immediately."

Noah bit his lip so hard it bled. He didn't want to leave Logan, not now, not ever. It was too soon, and he almost resented Hugh for the answer. Still, he understood what he had to do. "Today?"

He tried not to let his fear show, but his voice still trembled. Stubborn tears prickled at the corners of his eyes when the doctor confirmed Noah's words. "Yes. We can get you to the cryogenics facility within hours."

"Is that what you want to do, baby?" Logan asked quietly.

Noah nodded, because right now, he didn't think he could speak anymore. Logan picked him up in his arms, and they left the room. Raze and Uriel walked in front of them, and Doctor Wells followed in their wake. The formation proved to be on purpose, as Raze and Uriel distracted anyone who might have been too curious for their own good. Noah wondered what they thought. He wondered if he'd ever see them again. He didn't know where that thought had come from, but he couldn't shake it.

He was relieved when they at last reached the hangars. In complete silence, they slid into a hovercraft. Noah was a little confused, since he had expected the cryogenic facility to be here in Genesis. Apparently he'd been mistaken.

Raze guided the hovercraft out of the hangar and onto the streets of Genesis. Still in Logan's arms, Noah glimpsed out the window. He saw the large building he'd helped construct as the headquarters of the new Council, in the agora that had once held the Temple of Genesis. In an alarming twist, there were as many people there as had once gathered to see the Guiding Light.

Uriel must have guessed his confusion, because he turned toward Noah and explained, "They're cyborgs. These days I can't afford to travel, so we're flying people in to reboot their implants. It's a slow process, but it needs to be done."

Noah wanted to cry. Seeing the gathered crowd made him more aware than ever of the brewing war, and of the fact that he wouldn't be there for his loved ones. But if he didn't accept the cryo freeze, he'd be a burden for Uriel and Logan, and his unavoidable death would make an already bad situation worse.

"You're doing well, Uriel," he encouraged his brother. "Just remember not to strain yourself too much."

"He doesn't remember," Raze replied in Uriel's stead, "but I keep reminding him. Sometimes, it actually works. Don't worry, Noah. I'll be there for him."

That was indeed a relief, since Raze's loyalty and love toward Uriel rivaled Logan's toward Noah. Still, Noah might have asked more questions about what exactly was going on had the hovercraft not left Genesis altogether.

"Where are we going?" he decided to inquire. He feared they were headed toward the compound that had once been Uriel's so-called home. Noah's last visit there hadn't been pleasant.

Mercifully, whether he knew it or not, Uriel had anticipated this problem. "We built a separate facility, kind of like a refuge for important Edenian figures. I wasn't comfortable with returning to my previous one, and it wouldn't have been smart anyway since too many people knew about its existence. This is something smaller, and a guarantee that you'll be safe."

Judging by Uriel's words, it was more than that, possibly a hideout in case a war did start. The knowledge of Uriel's concern didn't come as a surprise, but for some reason, it still shook Noah.

Before Noah could express his worry, Raze elaborated on Uriel's words. "We made certain the refuge had an independent supply of energy and have assigned guards ordered to remain here at all times. My brother, Julian, has been overseeing everything personally when Uriel or I cannot. You'll be perfectly safe."

Noah suspected the words were more for Logan's benefit than his own. His lover was even tenser than Noah, which should have been impossible, but happened just the same. And the worst thing was that Noah could do absolutely nothing about it.

All too soon, they reached the refuge. Like Uriel's former home, it was an underground compound, but as soon as the hovercraft entered the hangars, Noah knew the resemblance stopped there. This was a place built with a very clear focus on technology. The purist tendency to disguise it under a façade of a supposedly glorious past was nowhere to be seen.

Noah's guess proved halfway correct. When they made their way out of the aircraft and into the actual structure, they found Raze's brother, Julian, waiting for them. Julian guided them through a maze of sleek corridors that were nonetheless spacious and created an airy feeling that relaxed Noah. Or maybe the relaxation came from the fact that Logan was still holding him. Noah couldn't be sure. Things always seemed so much better when Logan touched him.

Despite everything, the laboratory still made Noah uncomfortable. As soon as they entered it, Noah wanted to turn tail and flee. It was just like in his nightmares. He'd seen the genetics lab where he'd been created right before it had been destroyed, and the machinery here made the ghosts of his past reemerge.

To be fair, there were details in this laboratory that hadn't existed in the one haunting Noah's dreams. Elsewhere in the compound, Noah had seen no decorations, and while this could have easily been something he'd missed, he noticed it here. Of utmost note was the huge couch that dominated the center of the room and stood out for no apparent reason—no reason other than the fact that Uriel knew Noah so well.

Logan zeroed in on the couch at once and carried him there. As they settled down on the comfortable pillows, Hugh started to boot up the machines around them. Noah dared to ask the question that had been bothering him ever since Hugh had suggested this. "Do you have an estimate of how long it would take you to complete the research?"

Hugh didn't face him, but he did reply. "I'm sorry, I don't know. It could be a few months or a few years. There are too many factors involved for me to be able to give you an accurate assessment."

Noah's breath caught. A few years? That was too long, far too long. He looked at Logan, Logan who was trying to stay strong for him, to support him, to always be there for him.

"Logan... I want you to promise me something."

"Whatever you want, baby," Logan replied, as was his way.

"You mean the world to me, but if you find love with someone else, don't wait. Promise me that. Promise me you'll be happy."

It hurt to think of Logan in the arms of another, but Noah had already been selfish enough. If he was honest with himself, he could acknowledge he should have never existed, but despite his nightmares, he couldn't loathe himself as much as he had once, because Logan loved him. Logan had made him real, and had made him happy. He deserved a relationship that could fulfill him in turn.

Logan was already shaking his head, but Noah grabbed his hands and kissed them. "You know I'm right. You heard him. You have to give yourself the chance to love."

"I already love someone. You," Logan protested. "I can't forget that. Please don't ask me to."

It would have been cruel to insist, and it would have defeated Noah's purpose. He didn't want to make this about himself, about his own desire to know Logan happy and safe. "Very well. I won't. Just... keep it in mind. If you find happiness with someone else, you have my blessing."

Logan didn't acknowledge that, not that Noah expected him to. He cupped Noah's cheek with a gentleness that tore at Noah's heart. "I know what you're thinking, and I know you're blaming yourself for a million things that are not your fault. But I want you to promise me something as well. Always remember that you're the best thing that's ever happened to me. That will never change, no matter what. And even if you can't see me, even if we're apart, I will be there for you. I'll keep watch over you. You'll be safe."

Noah wanted to answer, but he didn't get the chance to come up with a reply that would adequately express the emotions bubbling inside him. Raze cleared his throat, interrupting their conversation. "You'll need to wear this."

He nodded toward a special jumpsuit Noah recognized as what was regularly used in such situations. The last thing Noah wanted was to change in front of all these people, but he felt thankful he even had the option. Oftentimes, cyborgs circumvented clothing altogether in the cryo freeze process. Noah didn't think he could have withstood that on top of everything else.

Mercifully, all those present except for Logan turned away. "Do you need help?" Logan asked him.

Noah shook his head. He wanted to at least maintain his dignity, and while he had no qualms to accept Logan's help when they were alone, with the others here it wasn't the same. "Let me try on my own."

It took far too long for him to pull on the jumpsuit over his flaking skin. His hands trembled, so he couldn't quite get a good grip on the material. In the end, Logan did help, albeit discreetly. Still, by the time he'd finished, Noah felt like he'd run a marathon, or stood in front of a crowd of believers as the Guiding Light.

It was a silly thought and a silly memory to come to him at a time like this, so he shook it off, focusing on the present instead. "All right. I'm done."

Hugh turned toward him once again. "We're ready here. Any moment you want, we can start the procedure."

Even with the warning they had received, Logan hesitated, having undoubtedly realized Noah's fears. Noah couldn't prolong this forever, and he took matters into his own hands. He got up and headed toward the cryogenics tube.

No one spoke, the weight of the moment a physical burden. Hugh pressed a few buttons, and the container opened. He offered Noah his hand to help him into the machine, but Noah ignored the man's offer. He entered the machine himself, even if his entire being was screaming to run in the other direction.

Inside, the tube held a platform meant to support Noah's body once he was in a horizontal position. Hugh placed Noah's arms against the platform, and Noah struggled to breathe, telling himself over and over that this was what he needed to do. "Ready?" the doctor asked.

Noah nodded, and as if on cue, restraints snapped around his wrists and legs. Noah's breath caught and he started to struggle, but Logan was immediately there, next to him. "It's okay, Noah. You're safe. Don't be scared. We're here for you."

The words soothed Noah and gave him the strength to remain inside the tube. Like a magic spell, they weaved around him, comforting him, keeping him from short-circuiting the device.

"That's it, Noah. Close your eyes. Sleep."

Noah complied. He heard the compartment close, but he clung to Logan's memory, to his promise. And then he slept.

Chapter Seven

THE THING about cryo freeze was that, unlike regular slumber, it didn't involve consciousness in any way. It wasn't really sleep, since there were no dreams, and thus, no nightmares. But there was also no process, no realization of the passage of time.

When he came to, Noah genuinely wondered why they'd woken him so quickly. He couldn't have been under for more than a few minutes. His vision was clouded, and he rubbed his eyes, noting with satisfaction that at one point, Hugh must have freed him from the restraints.

He then wondered if something had gone wrong. Had his bioenergy destroyed the machine, or had the doctor found different results, maybe making him incompatible with the cryogenics process?

As if hearing his unasked questions, Hugh manifested next to him and helped him out of the tube. "Hello, Noah. How do you feel?"

"Uh… I'm fine, I suppose…." Noah took a step forward, and his knees almost gave out. Hugh caught him before he could hit the floor. "All right, maybe I'm a bit dizzy."

"You needn't worry," Hugh told him. "This is a natural consequence of the cryogenic process. Your muscles have yet to recover from it."

Noah didn't want to think too much about that. He was too busy looking around the room. It looked pretty much the same, except for one significant difference. Uriel, Raze, and most importantly, Logan were nowhere to be seen.

He experienced a moment of severe disorientation. He could have sworn Logan had been standing right next to him mere instants ago. Sure, Logan could have stepped out. That made sense. That must have been what had happened.

He realized Hugh had been trying to talk to him when the doctor shook him. "Noah? Noah, can you hear me?"

"Yes, of course. I'm just…. Where's Logan? He was here a minute ago. Can you get him?"

Hugh didn't reply, steering him toward the couch instead. Noah went along with it solely because he couldn't fight back. "Doctor Wells? Please, can you get Logan?"

A different, unfamiliar voice answered his second inquiry. "Logan's not here. None of them are."

Noah turned so fast his head started to spin. A male figure stepped out from the shadows, and Hugh groaned. "I told you to be patient. I need time to—"

"Time? We don't have time, Hugh. If we could afford that luxury, we wouldn't be here in the first place."

Noah might not have recognized the voice, but he recognized its owner. Or at least, he thought he did. "Julian? Is that you?"

"You don't even recognize me anymore? I'm offended."

Julian sneered, and it looked out of place on him, or at least Noah deemed it so. Then again, he had changed in other ways. His hair was longer, and on his right side, it fell over his face, covering his eye and the better part of his cheek. He was dressed in an outfit very similar to what Raze usually wore. His previously slender build had become more toned, athletic. But what shocked Noah the most was that cold, disdainful expression. Noah and Julian had never been all that close, but the young man Noah had known was affectionate and caring. He'd loved his brother very much, and his friendship with Logan had guaranteed that Noah felt a degree of a distant bond to him. He'd also been among the few who'd supported Noah without question during Uriel's coma, and even after that.

Julian had also been mute when Noah had gone into cryo. Apparently his muteness had disappeared somewhere along the line,

91

much like his kindness. Not that it mattered. At this point, it was pretty obvious that no, Noah hadn't slept only a few minutes.

"How long was I in cryo?"

"Five years," Julian replied without preamble. "Well, four years and nine months. I haven't been keeping track of the exact days, I'm afraid."

His dismissive tone spoke volumes of how he felt about Noah, although Noah had no idea at what point and why Julian had started to resent him so. Then again, a lot of things could have happened in five years. Five years…. Oh, God. Logan. "Where's Logan?" he miraculously managed to breathe out. "What about Uriel? Where's my brother?"

If anything, Julian went even tenser. Hugh stopped him before he could reply. "Be patient. We'll tell you everything."

That didn't help at all, since Hugh's obvious concern increased Noah's panic. "Tell me now."

"Well, if you must know, Uriel and Raze are dead," Julian snapped at him. "As for Logan, he's missing. I hope that answered your questions."

Noah almost fainted. The world dimmed around the edges. He couldn't understand how everything he'd known had changed so quickly. Except it hadn't been quick, not at all. He'd just slept through it all.

Hugh intervened before Noah could panic even further. "Stop, Julian. You're not being helpful. We didn't come here for this."

"Why did you come?" Noah asked weakly. "Did you find the cure for me?"

Julian scoffed. "And there he is, caring solely about himself. I told you this was a poor idea."

Hugh ignored him. "Yes and no. Things happened, Noah, very unfortunate things."

"The war with Iberia? Abraham Zion?"

Julian smiled bitterly. "You know, thinking back, I'm almost nostalgic for a time when all we had to worry about was Iberia and Abraham. Of course, back then, I didn't realize the real threat came from within."

It didn't take a genius to make the connection between Julian's words and his attitude. It was Project Uriel. Somehow their secret had come out.

As far as he knew, Raze had never told his brother the truth about the genetically-engineered virus brought about by Uriel's mere existence. Only the four of them had known—Uriel, Noah, Raze, and Logan—and after that, Hugh Wells, enlisted to help Noah with his problem. Noah remembered the last words of the woman who by all accounts was the only mother he'd known. "Your secrets will be your downfall."

He'd hoped killing the Council members would silence those secrets, but he'd obviously been too optimistic. Something like that couldn't be buried forever, not with the amount of enemies Uriel and Noah had made.

Julian stalked to his side, the anger emanating off him like a palpable thing. "You know what I mean, don't you, Noah? You know what you did."

"Julian, back away," Hugh warned Raze's brother. "By now, we've more than established that Noah didn't do anything."

"How can you take their side, Hugh? You of all people should be aware of everything we've lost because of them. I truly thought Uriel was our savior. I thought, how wonderful he must be for giving me back my father. Little did I know that he was the one who took him away from me in the first place."

Despite his pain, or maybe because of it, Noah couldn't allow Julian to besmirch his brother's name. He shot to his feet, dizziness and weakness disappearing as anger took over.

"You still don't know anything, little man. You believe you do, but for all your self-righteousness, you don't understand Uriel, and you never will."

His bioenergy burned through his body, and electricity crackled at his fingertips. Julian's eyes widened and he paled, taking a hasty step back.

"Stop, Noah. This isn't helping, and you're only hurting yourself. Julian is angry and hurt. He isn't thinking straight. If he were, he'd never have said that."

Noah knew Hugh had a point, but he couldn't suppress the pain, the abject feeling of loss. He wanted to focus on the memory of Logan's promise to him, and to some extent, it worked. But Logan was missing too. He wasn't here to touch Noah and make him believe everything would be all right. His absence, coupled with the truth behind Julian's cruel words, pierced Noah's heart like sharp daggers, leaving him torn, desperate, furious, in agony.

He'd felt like this before, back when his nightmares had pushed him into becoming a killer. It was worse now, worse because once upon a time, he'd called the man in front of him friend, or at the very least, ally. Worse because Noah wanted to destroy him regardless. He wanted everyone to feel the pain he experienced, to know what it was like to lose his only anchor.

Julian had lost a brother too, but as far as Noah was concerned, that wasn't enough. Uriel had suffered so much, more than Julian could ever imagine. He'd been a victim, but he was always treated as if he'd contributed to the genocide on purpose.

Logan had been the only one—other than Raze, of course—to accept Uriel despite his misgivings. He'd admitted having those issues, but he'd learned to see past them. By the end, they'd even become friends, and that had been yet another reason why Noah had loved Logan. The memory added to Noah's pain, and he targeted Julian, fully intending to free himself from the agony by unleashing it upon his former ally.

Without a doubt, he'd have done exactly that, but in a gesture of supreme rashness and daring, Hugh reached for his arm again. The doctor held on, even if Noah suspected it hurt. His voice sounded strained as he spoke. "We're not sure Uriel is dead. Julian was unnecessarily blunt, but things are more complicated than he made them out to be. I need you to listen, if not for us, for Logan and for your brother."

Just like that, the wind went out of Noah's sails. He forgot all about Julian, smothered his pain, and focused on what the doctor was saying. "Tell me everything, Doctor. Please. I… I need to know."

Hugh nodded, the grimace of tension fading into something that almost seemed fond. "Five years ago, when you went into cryo, there was a lot of concern over Abraham Zion's loyalties. Uriel couldn't do much about it. The man had been disrespectful, but not treasonous, and imprisoning him without just cause would have made us no better than the previous political system. Raze and Logan took it upon themselves to discover this just cause. We all knew it was there. We just needed evidence."

"But it wasn't that easy, right?"

Hugh released a bitter chuckle. "Actually, it was. Zion hated Uriel so much that he made unfortunate decisions. In the end, we intercepted a communication between him and Condesa de la Vega, the diplomat who visited Genesis. You remember her."

Of course he did. For him, that visit had happened mere weeks before. Hugh must have realized that, because he continued to speak without waiting for a reply from Noah. "In any case, once that came out, we managed to apprehend Abraham. Uriel had words with the king of Iberia, and they agreed to a truce of sorts. Not that the guy had any right to it, but we didn't want to stir up conflict. After that... I suppose the next few years weren't that eventful. I kept looking for a cure for you, and made significant progress. In hindsight, I should have known something would go wrong."

"Why? If you were at peace, how did Uriel die?"

"We underestimated Abraham. He had more allies on his side than we thought he did. Somehow, he broke out of his prison. Later, it turned out that a member of our current Council had assisted him."

Noah cursed. He'd supported having purists on the Council, since at that time, the population had still been segregated and a ruling body made solely out of cyborgs would have unsettled the rest of the Edenians. Clearly, he shouldn't have trusted some of those people.

"Here it gets worse. We tracked him down to a facility three hundred miles from Genesis, hidden in the mountains. Apparently the property had belonged to your father and had been an unremarkable cabin. From our reports, Abraham hadn't been aware there was more to it either, and he was simply seeking refuge. He found more."

For the first time since Noah's outburst, Julian spoke. "There was an underground laboratory, with a crematorium attached. We soon realized this was the location where the purists had gone through with the original experiments to create Uriel. Or at least, Raze did. At the time, I had no idea what I was seeing, or what the purpose of the laboratory was. Abraham found the files, though, and he rejoiced in telling me all about it."

Noah winced. He could only imagine how that had gone. Abraham would have taken great pleasure in revealing the truth, to make Uriel suffer, to make him lose everyone he'd learned to love. Julian's attitude had angered Noah, but Uriel would have undoubtedly been hurt by it.

He didn't want to dwell on that frustration since, for the moment, Julian seemed to be on his side. He needed to know more about what had happened. His own resentment could wait.

"What did he do?"

"By then, he was furious with Uriel. He didn't care how many people he hurt as long as he got his revenge. Before our force could stop him, he released a broadcast that revealed the existence of Project Uriel to the entire world."

Noah gasped. "How could this happen? How could you let this happen?"

Julian glared back at him. "I was a little busy having my world torn apart. Besides, no one expected he could even do that from the middle of nowhere. Raze and Logan wanted to take him down without having to hurt him, but by the time they managed to sneak in, he'd already gone through with his plan. And after that, everyone was so shocked he almost shot me."

Further recriminations were futile. Noah hadn't been there to help, so he couldn't in good conscience point fingers. Undoubtedly, Raze and Logan had done everything in their power to prevent disaster. In the end, even if Abraham hadn't revealed the secret when he had, it would have come out eventually.

"I take it people didn't react well."

"You could say that." Hugh directed him to the console. "But maybe you should see it for yourself."

96

The doctor activated the screen and as it flared to life, an image of Uriel appeared. He stood in front of a gathering of unfamiliar men and women, with Raze by his side.

"We demand retribution," a blond man dressed in a military uniform snarled. "Do you have any concept of the number of people you killed?"

"Actually, yes," Uriel replied coolly. "It's not something I can ever forget. However, I must note that I am hardly to blame for the situation, since I was only a newborn at the time."

"Permit me to disagree," an Asian woman with a tight bun answered. "We are not here to argue semantics, and no matter what you might say, you are guilty of crimes against humanity. You must be punished."

"When was this?" Noah asked, shaking. "Where?"

"All world powers agreed on a meeting in Iberia, three months ago," Hugh explained. "Ironically, Iberia's truce with Eden remained in place despite the new situation, and they agreed to hold the meeting there."

Noah couldn't believe his ears. "And Raze and Uriel went? They trusted those people?"

"You speak as if they had much of a choice," Julian said bitingly. "And for the record, Logan was there too."

Noah dropped on the nearby chair, his knees refusing to hold him up. He didn't want to look, didn't want to see the unavoidable betrayal. But he did look, even if he dreaded the moment when he'd see Raze's death and his brother's downfall.

As it turned out, none of what he expected happened. During his conversation with Hugh and Julian the video had continued, and the meeting had predictably dissolved into more insults directed toward Uriel. All the while, Uriel faced them without faltering. And when they finally stopped speaking, he took over the conversation.

"I had moments in the past during which I experienced the guilt you would have me feel. And even now, I will always carry the burden of the blood others painted on my hands. But you would have me pay for these crimes—these crimes that I am not actually guilty of—with my life. I refuse. Not because I am a coward. Not even because I don't wish to leave the man I love alone. But because I know that the moment I am gone, all of you will turn against Eden. All of you will become just as bad as my would-be parents were. And you will destroy my people. You will destroy each other. There will be more war, more death, more pain, and that I cannot allow." He paused, looking at each individual face without flinching. "I do not wish to make threats. I have only ever wanted to rebuild this world. That does not mean I will bow down and let you take over. You direct your hate at me now, but once I am gone, what would you do? I cannot take back what the purist regime in Eden did, but I am trying to fix what can be fixed. And if you want the good of your people, you'll help me."

Noah had never felt more proud of Uriel. He had feared in his heart that Uriel had allowed these people their revenge, because it was a revenge they both deemed justified. But Uriel seemed to have learned to live with the past, and Noah suspected Raze had helped him with that. Uriel might have said Raze was not the reason he wanted to live, but that was the one thing in the entire speech that Noah doubted.

He didn't expect wonders to happen after it, and indeed, the meeting erupted in more angry comments and never-ending debates. And then someone reached for Uriel's arm. It was a stupid thing, really. Raze was right there and would have been able to eviscerate the foolish individual in moments. As it turned out, he didn't have to, because the man—the prime minister of a country in the Middle East, if Noah remembered correctly—fell back as electricity crackled through the air. Uriel's eyes shone brightly, and the video cut off.

Noah couldn't help but feel a burst of panic, but Hugh quickly soothed him. "Uriel's power just killed the system, but nothing worse happened. Turns out that man did us a favor, and the world leaders learned Uriel was to be feared. Or maybe, they were reminded of it. And they were too afraid to do anything while still unprepared."

"So it wasn't them? They didn't hurt Uriel? What happened to him, then?"

"Well, this is another thing you should see, but in person. Do you think you can walk?"

Noah was still unsteady on his feet. Now that he'd managed to suppress his outburst, the energy he'd used nauseated him. But he had to know. Besides, judging by Hugh's words, this entire thing had happened months, if not weeks before now. If Hugh had chosen to awaken him, it was for a reason.

Maybe he could help. Julian had said they were running out of time. If things had been beyond hope, surely that wouldn't have come into question at all.

He didn't want to hope, but he still clung to his decision as he nodded. "I'll be fine. Show me."

"In a minute," Hugh said, earning himself a glare from Julian.

The demanded minute turned out to be necessary. Hugh used it to retrieve a vial of serum from a nearby container and inject it into Noah's arm. Noah felt a little more clearheaded after that, which was a good thing, because the other two men were already in motion. They left the room, guiding him through the same corridors Logan had carried him through. If the passage of time hadn't been obvious before, Noah would have definitely noticed now. Everything was darker, dustier. The very air seemed to weigh on him. Was he imagining it? Perhaps. But even after the video he'd seen, he had trouble reconciling the intellectual knowledge with how cryo freeze had affected him. In the blink of an eye, he'd lost everyone he'd ever loved.

No, not everyone, not yet. Logan had promised to be there for him, and that promise remained in place. It went both ways, and neither of them would let go, not until they stopped drawing breath. As for Uriel.... Noah didn't know yet, but he hoped he'd soon find out.

They stopped only briefly in a small room where Noah found a change of clothes and a few toiletries. After he was clean and dressed, they headed out once again. The guards who'd kept watch over the area had disappeared. A lone, battered hovercraft waited in the hangars. The lights flickered as the three of them entered it.

"I thought you were going to show me what happened to Uriel."

Hugh didn't look at him as he activated the controls of the aircraft. "I am."

They shot out of the hangar and to the surface. After the dimness of the underground compound, Noah had to close his eyes at the bright light that assaulted him. Julian was not impressed. "Don't shy away. I thought you wanted to see your brother."

It wasn't the dismissive words that made Noah open his eyes, though. It was the scream, so loud, so piercing, reaching out to Noah's very soul. Noah looked, and what he saw made him want to scream in turn.

From outside the compound, he should have been able to see Genesis. The great city was no longer there. Instead, a huge vortex of energy had appeared, and the waves of power seemed to draw ever nearer.

In one of the waves, a familiar figure materialized. Uriel reached out to Noah. "Help me! Noah, please help me."

Noah almost jumped out of the hovercraft. He was halfway out of it when Julian grabbed his arm and dragged him back in. "What do you think you're doing? Do you want to die?"

"Why do you think we got you out, Noah?" Hugh asked. "The vortex will be swallowing the compound within hours, and the energy inside it can kill you."

"No." Noah shook his head. "Uriel would never do that to me."

"Your brother is gone," Hugh said sadly. "He... he saw Raze die. There was a cyborg woman. I'd known her for years. Her name was Odette. I should have realized she wouldn't take kindly to what she'd learned."

"She had two children, a little younger than me," Julian added tightly. "We used to play together. I don't remember them much anymore, but I do remember their dead bodies."

Noah couldn't say anything anymore. He thought he might remember the cyborg woman they were talking about. She'd been close to Raze, loyal, and she'd had faith that Raze was doing the right thing. In fact, Uriel had once told Noah she'd formed part of the group that had come to save him from the purist underground compound.

"She tried to kill Uriel," Julian elaborated. "Raze got in the way. No one could have survived Odette's shot, not even him. And Uriel... broke."

Hugh was already flying away, taking advantage of Noah's distraction to put distance between them and the vortex. Noah didn't have the patience to hear anymore. "Stop talking like that. Don't you see him? Uriel's right there."

Julian gave him a telling look. "I don't see anything. What do you mean?"

Noah turned to follow Julian's gaze, only to realize his brother's image had disappeared. "He was there," he whispered. "He said my name. He asked me to help him."

"Noah, don't." Hugh turned away from the controls long enough to glare at him. "Trying to enter that place would be like signing your own death warrant. Do I have to repeat myself? Uriel's energy will destabilize your cell structure. It would destroy you. It's not about intent, but about fact, and the fact is that there were a million people in Genesis during the assassination. Not one of them came out of the vortex. This is the virus all over again."

"And if he absorbs your bioenergy, he will be unstoppable," Julian snapped. "There's nothing left of your brother, not really. He'll kill us all. We can't allow that."

So that was the real reason they'd come for him, not out of a particular fondness or the hope that he could help, but because letting him stay here would have made things worse. Given the circumstances, they'd probably been unable to move the cryogenics facility in time, or perhaps they hadn't cared one way or another.

Either way, he knew in his heart that they were wrong. Uriel was physically alive. If he'd died, the bioenergy would have disappeared with him. But they were arguing against the existence of Uriel's consciousness as the force that controlled it.

Noah hadn't been there the day of the assassination, but he could empathize. If he'd seen Logan die in his arms, he would have broken too. Hell, he'd been very close to an outburst of his own. But he also knew his brother was strong, stronger than any of them believed and gave him credit for.

If Uriel had been the only person he loved, Noah wouldn't have hesitated. He'd have forced the hovercraft to land and gone in search of his brother. But there was Logan, the most important man in Noah's life. Noah couldn't abandon him, not even for Uriel.

He looked back toward the vortex of energy. "Was Logan there when it happened?"

Julian shook his head. "He was here, at the compound." A bitter smile. "He was always here, when he and Raze weren't out on some sort of mission. I suppose I should be thankful. In a way, your existence, as regrettable as it might be, saved his life."

In that moment, Noah realized it. He'd thought the only reason behind Julian's anger was Uriel's involvement in the virus, but he'd been wrong.

Julian didn't love Logan as a brother, but as a man. He was jealous, and his jealousy had festered in his heart for five years.

Noah remembered his final conversation with Logan. Had Logan started a relationship with Julian, however brief? The thought made him ache, but at the same time, he almost wished that was the case. He didn't want to imagine Logan waiting for him, standing in that laboratory, staring at his frozen form, unable to touch.

He might have apologized to Julian, but he decided their emotions were irrelevant right now. Logan hadn't been in Genesis. So he'd survived the day of the assassination. What had happened to him then?

As if guessing his thoughts, Julian explained, "Since Uriel's death, we've been trying to stabilize the country. There was an attack in Canaan. Logan and I went to handle it. I never figured out who they were working for, but by the end of the battle, Logan had disappeared."

Noah had expected something like that, but it still didn't make the words any easier to hear. "All right. Let's find Logan."

Even as he spoke, he kept staring at the shining whirlpool of energy where Genesis had once been. "Forgive me, brother. I'll come back for you. I promise."

In the glowing rays at the very edge of the vortex, he thought he saw Uriel's smile.

THEY TOOK to him to a nondescript warehouse that seemed torn from every briefing he'd ever had about being taken captive by enemy troops. Logan had struggled, and he had taken out a good number of the mercenaries. But he'd been heavily outgunned and even more heavily outnumbered, so he'd resigned himself to the captivity, at least for the moment.

He immediately started making plans to escape, but putting those ideas into practice would have been easier if the first thing they did wasn't to drug him out of his wits. For a while, he wasn't even conscious, and he only recovered when they were already at the damn warehouse, so he didn't even know where he was.

After that, faceless technicians stepped in. They strapped him to a machine and pinned sensors to him, and Logan struggled once more, because he knew what those sensors did. He'd worked with something similar while designing the VR, and hell no, they could torture him as much as they wanted, but they were not getting a free pass into his mind.

One moment, he lay there, strapped to the machine and attempting to fight it with all his might, and the next, he was free. The weight of the phaser in his hand felt comforting. He remembered he had a mission to do, something very important he'd come here for.

His vision cleared and Abraham Zion stood in front of him, next to a computer console. "Back away from the console now." Logan steadied his phaser and aimed it at the fugitive who'd given them more trouble than he was worth. "Come quietly, and we can still find a nonviolent way to deal with your imprisonment."

Abraham turned slowly and faced Logan, not seeming in the least bit intimidated. "Is that right? Somehow I don't particularly believe your reassurances."

Julian took a step forward. It was against Logan's good judgment, since he would have preferred it if Julian hadn't been there at all. However, Julian was the one who'd tracked Abraham down to begin with, and he wasn't a child any longer. In some ways, he was better at handing politicians than Logan and even Raze, mostly because three-quarters of them deemed him harmless.

"I know you and Uriel haven't always seen eye to eye," Julian said softly, "but he has only ever attempted to do what was best for Eden—and that includes you."

Abraham burst into laughter. "Do you truly believe that? My God, you do. You don't even know who the man you support truly is."

Julian blinked in surprise, and a cold shiver swept over Logan's spine. Abraham continued, undeterred. "I've never made that mistake. I always knew your Uriel was a monster." He smirked, his eyes glinting with a maniacal light. "Now the whole world will know it too."

"No...." Raze gasped. "What have you done?"

"I believe you already know, Mr. Hartman," Abraham said. "Uriel was the virus, and now everyone will see that."

Behind him, the console flared to life, depicting an image of Uriel's DNA with the words Project Uriel written above it. Julian's breath caught and his gaze went to his brother, then to Logan. He was obviously seeking reassurance, wanting them to tell him this was a lie. But Logan didn't have the calm or the presence of mind to muster up even the flimsiest of excuses. All he could think about was that he'd failed Noah. He'd been unable to protect Uriel. He'd fucked up, and Eden would pay the price.

Abraham reached for his phaser, already pointing it at Julian. Why he'd decided to target Julian was anyone's guess, but Logan's self-deprecating thoughts slid aside, replaced by the urgency of battle. He didn't hesitate. He activated his phaser, and the plasma bolt struck Abraham straight in the chest.

The man's body jerked and he dropped his weapon. He crumpled to the floor and went still. Raze was by his side in seconds, checking his pulse. When he shook his head at Logan, Logan had to admit he was surprised. His phaser had been set on stun. They hadn't wanted more death, which was why Abraham had been alive despite the evidence of his plotting. But his advanced senses confirmed Raze's conclusions. Logan wished he could have regretted it. Instead, he just felt cold and empty.

104

Steadying himself, he headed toward the console and checked the files that had been transmitted. What he saw confirmed his worst fears. Project Uriel had been exposed to the world.

Despite this being a remote location, the computer contained a backup of all the purists' files. In fact, the backup was so thorough he even found a folder named Project Regenesis—a reference to Noah's cloning most likely. He accessed it in numb horror, and what he found inside shocked him to the core. The original virus hadn't been enough for the purists. They'd managed to come up with a second wave, a retooling of the original process that used implants within their own bodies to create a mind-controlling effect within the remaining cyborgs.

Uriel and Raze's intervention had interrupted them from completing their plan, but the implants had been there, a ticking time bomb that could have gone off at any moment... if Noah hadn't killed them.

Had Noah known about it? He must have, even if he'd never mentioned it. In a way, it made so much sense, because despite Noah's emotional instability, Logan had never seen his lover as a cold-blooded killer.

Logan was still struggling to process the information when he heard Julian come up behind him. He turned to look at his friend as Julian pressed his hand on his shoulder. "You can't do this any longer, Logan," Julian whispered, eyes pleading. "You can't waste away waiting for him. He's never coming back."

Logan narrowed his eyes at Julian, the words stirring something angry and dark inside him. If they'd come from someone else, he would have punched the foolish individual in question. But he and Julian were still close, and Logan loved him, even if not in the way Julian wanted.

"This is my choice, Julian," he replied with as much calm as he could muster. "I cannot just forget the man I love. Besides, it wouldn't be fair for anyone if I tried to enter another relationship."

Julian leaned against his chest, his smile both hopeful and sensual. "I don't care about fairness. Come on, Logan. Let me take care of you for once."

Logan's breath caught at the look in Julian's dark eyes. He hated himself because he was tempted. Julian had been like a little brother to him, but in past years, since Noah had been frozen, he'd grown from the shy young man Logan had known. And Logan had moments when he missed Noah so much, when the pain and the yearning became so profound he couldn't bear it. The loneliness threatened to crush him, and he couldn't go to Raze, because seeing Uriel would make it worse.

So Logan had turned to Julian. He'd only realized his mistake that night, two months ago, when Julian had leaned over the table and kissed him.

For a few seconds, Logan had kissed him back. It had been four years since he'd lost Noah to cryo freeze, and he hadn't taken anyone to bed since then. Sometimes he felt as cold as Noah must be in that tube.

Naturally, he'd come to his senses, but by then, the damage was done. Julian knew there was attraction between them, and Logan felt like a heel. He was both betraying Noah and using Julian.

Things hadn't changed since then, and this time around, Logan gripped Julian's wrists and steadily pushed him away. "No, Jules. You know as well as I do it would be a mistake, just like that kiss. You deserve better than a man who loves another."

Julian's lips thinned. "So what now? You heard Hugh. No matter how hard he tries, he can't find a cure. Noah might be a person, but he's also a clone. Will you abandon all your chances to be happy for someone who'll dissipate in your arms?"

Pain rushed through Logan at the memories those words evoked. Noah had tried so hard, but in the end, he'd been unable to fight what he couldn't help. And Logan had been crushed to see him fall apart, physically and mentally.

He pushed Julian away so hard the man staggered and fell back. Under different circumstances, Logan might have felt guilty about it, but Julian had hurt him. And it was his own fault, for encouraging this even a little, but that didn't make it any less painful.

Without looking at Julian, he rushed into the lab. He found Noah in the cryogenic container, and the sight filled him with both pain and relief. Julian had stirred his most secret fears, that one day he'd come here and find the equipment had malfunctioned. Noah would feel trapped in that compartment. He'd panic. It would make him feel ill. From that point on, all sorts of grim scenarios emerged in his mind, and the only way to quiet them was to come here.

Logan pressed his hand to the glass of the container, watching his lover's unconscious form. To him, Noah looked as beautiful as ever, even if he wasn't quite the same. His hair was completely white now, cut short out of necessity. Logan missed the golden blond waves. For the most part, the serum had stopped the aging of his skin, but Logan knew that if they'd waited any longer, Noah would have been dead by now.

As he thought this, something niggled at the back of his mind, something that didn't quite make sense. Now? When was now? What was happening?

Hadn't he been fighting Abraham Zion just moments ago? Why.... No, this didn't make sense. He turned toward the door, ready to leave the lab. He had to return to Genesis to.... What had Raze asked him to do? He couldn't remember.

No, he didn't want to remember. This was all wrong. He shouldn't be here, shouldn't be seeing this, reliving this. He struggled against the memory, pushing it to the back of his mind where no one else could touch it. It was his, like his feelings for Noah. They had no right, no right to steal it, no right to burrow into his mind and see all of his regrets.

As he fought, the sound of voices reached his ears. "Madam, he's resisting." It was the technicians, damn it, those mercenaries who'd captured him.

"Do we have the information we need?" a woman asked.

"No, not yet. The memory wasn't clear enough. It didn't provide the location of the subject."

"Well, keep trying," the woman snapped. She sounded familiar. Why did she sound familiar? Logan couldn't tell. Maybe he was imagining things.

"If we probe deeper now, we risk breaking his mind. He's more resilient than expected."

"Of course he is." The answer came as if between gritted teeth. "After all, that is why he was chosen."

Logan tried to open his eyes, the exchange giving him strength, fueling the resistance that irritated these people so much. They wanted something from him, and if Logan had to guess, it was connected to Noah.

His efforts must have been noticed, because an alarmed voice squeaked, "He's regaining consciousness. We can't hold him under."

"Fools! Ignore the probe. Just make sure he doesn't wake. And someone get me Julian. I need answers, and I need them now. I will not...."

The rest of what the woman said was drowned out as Logan was plunged back into the darkness.

Chapter Eight

THE HOUR was late when they reached Canaan. The small town was quiet, abandoned after the battle that had destroyed several buildings and left the rest scorched and with no utilities.

Noah couldn't imagine why any foreign force would choose to strike here of all places. Canaan was a peaceful settlement, with no real connections to the political entanglements of Genesis. It held no secrets, at least nothing important enough to draw negative attention. The only thing remarkable about it was that it wasn't remarkable at all. Now it was noticeable if only because of the ominous silence.

Noah wondered if there was any point to him being here at all. Hugh and Julian had brought him to Canaan in the hope of finding a clue to Logan's whereabouts, but if there had been anything to find, it was long gone now.

Well, they needed to start somewhere. As they left the hovercraft to explore the place where Julian had last seen Logan, Noah struggled to come up with a plan.

"You still don't know who caught him?"

"Foreign nations deny all involvement," Julian replied. "The identifications we lifted from the bodies suggest the attacking force was formed of mercenaries, but the brains behind the operation…. That's a mystery."

"Any particular nationality on the mercs?"

"They were from all over the place. Europe, Asia, even Africa."

Noah scowled. "No one from Eden?"

"Not as far as we could tell. As a rule, Logan is still well liked among other cyborgs, so I gather whoever attacked would've had trouble finding someone loyal to them."

"There's always the possibility that there were Edenian mercs in the group," Hugh offered. "But we didn't catch them."

Well, that didn't help at all. "What could they want with Logan?" Noah asked, only half addressing the question to his companions, trying to untangle the mess. Uriel might not have had an active role in leading Eden, but he was educated in politics, largely through his own efforts. So through his brother's memories, Noah had some knowledge of how this worked. But even without that information, he could be logical about this. He had to, because if he started panicking, Canaan would be engulfed in a vortex of energy too, and that wouldn't help anyone.

"Raze is dead," he mused to himself. "Logan's importance to Eden largely stemmed from his connection to Raze. We can't assume someone wanted to hold him for ransom, because if that had been the case, we'd have already heard something, right?"

Julian's silence didn't surprise him, since Noah hadn't been very considerate when it came to his feelings regarding his brother. Hugh, however, provided his own opinion. "Logan is still important. He was in the inner circle of the Guiding Light for years. It's likely that his kidnapper is after whatever secrets Logan might have to tell him."

"I don't think there are too many secrets left to reveal," Noah replied sarcastically.

"There's you," Julian said. "At this point, you're the only remnant of the Guiding Light, and your DNA holds the secret to the cure for the virus-related injuries. But you have been officially declared dead, so I'm not sure who'd try to find you after all this time."

"Dead?" Noah repeated in disbelief. That was an interesting little tidbit they hadn't shared until now.

Hugh nodded. "There was a funeral service and everything. Uriel and Logan agreed it would be safest for people to think you were dead. After all, it would be easy to deny it once you recovered."

"And people believed it?"

"Of course." Julian scoffed. "They were already making assumptions when you disappeared after that day Logan brought you to the mansion. You weren't in the best shape, and people noticed. It was actually how Uriel and Logan came up with the idea."

That made sense, although it bothered Noah that both his brother and his lover had been forced to mourn him in public. Too late to do anything about it now.

"Technically speaking, the guards at the compound could have told anyone," he said, instead of dwelling on the many things he couldn't change. "I'm betting their loyalties took a hit when Project Uriel was revealed."

Julian chuckled bitterly. "Yes, except Raze handpicked those guards. Most of them had fought by Raze's side before the virus struck. All of them, without exception, had mental computers, and it wasn't difficult for Uriel to wipe that little tidbit from their minds."

"Uriel wouldn't do something like that," Noah snapped. "You're lying."

Such manipulation went against everything Uriel believed in, more so because Noah had suffered a form of it when he'd had Uriel's memories implanted. Hugh gave him an almost sad look. "No, he isn't. It's true that Uriel tried to talk to them but... they weren't exactly receptive. I truly believe that some of them would have broken into the facility and killed you with their own hands in retribution for what happened."

Judging by Julian's expression, he probably agreed with that assessment. In Julian's angry eyes, Noah saw all the other citizens of Eden, and he realized Hugh was probably telling the truth.

Noah remembered the steel in Uriel's voice from when his brother had spoken at the international meeting, and he flinched. He knew how hard it must have been for Uriel to go through with something like that. His brother must have been pushed to the extreme to make that choice, but as the vortex had eloquently proven, this was a very extreme situation. There were many things Raze had been unable to protect him from.

"But someone might have suspected it and taken Logan because he would know where I was."

Julian and Hugh gave him glum looks that told him they agreed. It was the worst situation imaginable. Of course, Julian and Hugh must have already figured it all out. Was that the real reason they'd taken him out of cryo, or maybe a second one?

"You want to use me to lure whoever took Logan, maybe exchange him for me. Is that it?"

Julian didn't even blink. "Look, Noah, I'll speak plainly. Logan is a soldier. He'll resist whatever methods these people have. But I'm fairly certain they'd do mental probing of some sort, and that…. Well, it's not something anyone has many defenses against. Once they find their answer and realize you're not even where you're supposed to be, they might lash out and kill him. So we have to go through with this."

Noah narrowed his eyes at them. "You already spoke with this person. That's why we're here."

Julian threw his hands in the air. "You're kidding, right? If we wanted to sell you out, we wouldn't have bothered to thaw you to begin with."

"But that is your plan nonetheless." Noah couldn't even blame them. He just wished they stopped telling him only bits and pieces. The less he knew, the more likely it was that they'd fail in their endeavor to help Logan.

Noah bit his lip and looked from Julian to Hugh. "Can you craft me the cure? I might need my powers to escape."

Hugh shook his head. "I don't have everything I need for it, and I never got the chance to complete my research."

Just like that, Noah knew he'd made a grave error. He couldn't trust them. Whether there was a cure or not, they'd never share it with him. Hugh might not hate him, but he did hate Uriel, and that in itself made him Noah's enemy. While they'd been in control of the situation, he had no doubt that the doctor had genuinely helped him, but five years had passed, and things had changed.

As for Julian, it was more than obvious that he didn't want Noah to escape. If Noah's guess was right, it must have been Hugh who'd made the decision to thaw Noah. At this point, he wouldn't put it past Julian to want to hand him over like a thing or a lab rat.

Maybe he was wrong. Maybe he was seeing things through the filter of his own emotional instability. But in this, he knew he only had one ally, the person he'd left behind in a vortex of energy.

Uriel understood. Uriel would always understand, because Raze was just as important to him as Logan was to Noah. And it would be cruel of Noah to ask him for his help, but maybe they could find a way to help each other.

No, he was fooling himself. What could Uriel possibly do for him now? He had to admit the truth. If he risked following this plan, Logan would be free, especially since Julian seemed to have a romantic interest in him. But he'd have to abandon his brother to his fate. The whole point of this endeavor was for Julian to save Logan, but also to get rid of Noah. He wasn't fool enough to believe they'd allow anyone to gain control of him and his priceless DNA.

In the end, he had no choice. He plopped down next to a crumbling wall. "Well, what are you waiting for? Do what you came here to do. I'm not going to run."

Julian had the gall to look surprised. "Truly?"

"Of course. I want Logan safe. I prize him more than my own life." He smiled sadly. "I don't know if you're aware, but before I went into cryo freeze, I told Logan he could be happy with someone else, that he shouldn't wait for me. It's sad to see the person who could have given him that only has this crippled, wrecked thing to offer."

Julian went rigid and reached for his phaser, but Hugh gripped his arm before the other man could retrieve his weapon. "Stop. Don't do this. Now is not the time."

"Didn't you hear what he said?"

"I heard, but it doesn't mean anything. He doesn't understand. He's just a clone, remember?"

Noah almost laughed. He'd told himself that more times than he could count, but he now realized the way he'd been brought into this world didn't matter. "I might be a clone, but I love Logan. And

113

if you really loved him, Julian, you'd know that hurting me will hurt him in turn."

Julian said nothing. There was nothing *to* say, because they both knew Noah was right. Julian didn't want him to be, but it was a truth that could not be denied. Funny how Noah had only realized his own worth now, when it was too late.

He took a deep breath, pushing back the panic and frustration he knew originated from his condition. He was not dead yet, and whether or not Julian and Hugh wanted him to be so, he owed it to Logan and Uriel to try his best to stay alive. But these so-called allies of his didn't need to know that.

He closed his eyes and slumped his shoulders, hoping to convey an image of utmost despair. "It doesn't matter anyway. I'm going to die, and you'll have Logan all to yourself. I only wish you deserved him." He didn't even have to fake the crack in his voice, and that helped.

"Look, Noah, Eden is gone," Hugh said. "It's time for everyone to start over. This is for the best. You owe at least this much to the world."

Noah nodded, even if what he truly wanted to do was to summon his ability and lash out. He owed them nothing. The only people who could claim anything from him were Logan and Uriel, and anyone else who presumed to control him would find themselves facing a very unfortunate surprise.

"Make the deal," he said softly. "I'll cooperate."

"Well, for the moment we're stuck waiting. One of the mercs contacted us and said they'd make the exchange here."

Noah opened his eyes and stared at the two men in disbelief. Just a few minutes ago, they'd claimed they'd had no contact with the kidnappers. Did they even know what they were saying, or had they lost their sense of truth somewhere along the way? It was sad to see, since it contrasted so sharply with the memory Noah had of Julian.

Five years. Five years gone in a heartbeat, and Noah had lost so much. Friends. Family. Hope. And to think, it had all been for naught, because the cure was as elusive as it had been the day he'd gone into cryo.

What would have happened if he'd refused Hugh's idea and resisted cryogenics? Where would Logan be now? Perhaps he'd have let go of the past and started a new life with Julian.

Logan. Uriel. Raze. Memories flashed through his mind, images of time spent together, laughter, tears, comfort, and affection. Uriel and Raze had been so in love too. Now Raze was dead. Noah still didn't know the details of that particular event beyond what little Julian had told him. Even so, nothing else could have triggered such an outburst from Uriel. It occurred to him that a lot of Julian's anger was directed at himself.

"You abandoned him, didn't you?" he asked. "You abandoned Raze."

He hadn't thought Julian could get any tenser, but all the color drained from his face, leaving him as pale as a corpse. Something dark and angry twisted inside Noah. "You were here. You could have helped them. But you didn't. You got so hung up on the past that you didn't care about the present. And in the end, you lost it all."

"Noah...." Hugh started to say, a warning in his tone.

"He has to hear it. I'm dying, Hugh, but I would have given anything to be able to support Uriel and Logan. And it's not the same, I know it's not the same, but shouldn't love be stronger than hate?"

At his question, Julian recovered and scoffed. "Look around you, Noah. That's a fairy tale. Love means nothing."

"Indeed," a voice said from the shadows. "I completely agree."

An unfamiliar figure stepped out into the light, and Hugh gasped in shock. "You... it's not... it's not possible."

The woman smiled, a viper coming out to strike and reveling in the poison she was about to release. "You should know by now, Hugh. There are few things in this world that are impossible."

Noah got up steadily, watching the approach of this unknown foe. Julian took a step forward, ignoring the exchange between Hugh and the woman. "I don't know who the hell you are, but that man you sent told me you'd free Logan if I brought you the clone. Here he is. Release Logan."

The woman tutted, the waves of her dark hair falling to frame her face. Noah had the strangest feeling he'd seen her somewhere before, although that couldn't be right. If he had, he'd have definitely remembered. Snakes that took the shape of people were pretty remarkable.

"So impatient, my darling," she said. "Not to worry. I didn't harm your beloved. Much."

She waved her hand and two masked men emerged from the shadows, carrying the very still body of Logan. They dumped him at her feet, but didn't move away, obviously aware of the danger Logan could still pose.

"Logan!"

Both Noah and Julian cried out at the same time and moved forward together, for once in agreement about what they wanted to do. The woman tsked. "You're aware of the deal, Noah, are you not? I'll return Logan as long as you come with me. Quietly."

It wasn't his deal to begin with, but the look Hugh gave the woman told Noah he might have to go along with it. Most importantly, Logan needed medical attention, and Noah's hesitation wouldn't help him now.

"I understand," he said with a nod. "But I don't trust you to return him if I agree to come with you."

The woman scoffed. "I don't need him now that I've found what I've been looking for."

"You could use him against me. You know I love him."

The woman chuckled. "Brave. Daring. Perhaps too much. Does that come with living with the proverbial Sword of Damocles hovering over you? Or is it just who you are?"

"I don't know." Noah shrugged, affecting a nonchalance he really did not feel. This woman knew too much about him, and he'd already guessed that. It didn't mean he was comfortable with it. "Does it matter?"

"I suppose it doesn't." She smiled, and her eyes glittered with something like a promise. "You're right. I would use Logan against you if you force my hand. You need help."

Noah had expected anything except that. At first, he just stared at her, but then he realized she was serious. "And you'll give it to me?"

"Of course." She grinned. "I can help you. I can save your life."

Noah burst into laughter. "Do you think I am a fool? You took Logan. You hurt him. That makes you my enemy. If you believe an empty promise will make me trust you, you're not as intelligent as you seem."

"I don't require your trust, just your cooperation." She flicked her fingers, and one of the men holding Logan maneuvered him to his knees and retrieved a phaser. As the mercenary placed the weapon to Logan's temple, the woman arched a brow. "Come toward me. Slowly."

Noah gritted his teeth. "All right. I'll do what you want. Just let Logan go."

In that moment, the most unexpected thing happened. Logan regained consciousness. He didn't immediately open his eyes, but Noah knew Logan, and he was able to tell. He studiously looked away from Logan, hoping his tension would not give away his lover's plan. "Put him down," he added, "and I'll come with you."

The woman sighed, now sounding irritated. "Let's stop this ridiculous game. I said I would, didn't I? Now, come. We need to go. You're running out of time, and your anxiousness over Logan isn't doing you any favors. At this rate, you'll start disintegrating before I can do anything about it."

Logan's eyes snapped open, and he shoved off the two mercenaries who had been keeping him trapped. The motion dislodged the phaser placed against his temple. He moved so quickly that before anyone could do anything about it, he was on his feet, having already grabbed the weapon and shot the mercs.

The woman was already shouting, though, and more people emerged from the building. Countless mercenaries pointed their weapons at Logan, and Noah couldn't take it anymore. It was too easy to remember Uriel's pain and despair, too easy to imagine himself in that position, Logan dead and forever lost to him. No matter what happened to him, he couldn't allow it. He had to save Logan.

The power burst out of him, wild and angry, his only control over it his grief and his need to protect Logan. It zeroed in on the mercenaries, and there were shouts all around as the men and women received a nasty dose of electricity as punishment. The leader of the group wasn't spared, although oddly enough, she seemed more resilient than her underlings.

Nonetheless, Noah could have easily killed them all. He'd done it before. But he didn't want to do it now, not again, and not in front of Logan.

So he reeled back his power, trapping it inside him with the knowledge that he'd helped and Logan was free to go now.

The next thing he knew he was lying on the ground, staring up at his lover. "Hang in there, Noah. We'll find you help. Breathe for me."

Noah breathed deeply. The warmth of Logan's arms made him feel safe, and for the first time since waking up in this strange new reality, things fell into place. Tears trailed down his cheeks, but he let them fall. Everything was okay now. Logan was okay, and somehow, they'd reach Uriel too. When Logan held him, Noah could believe that and more.

The unknown woman knelt next to him, a strangely sedate expression on her face. "How is he?" she asked.

"Weak." Logan's voice was so low it could have come from the grave. "Move aside. I need to take him someplace else."

"No one and nothing can help him, except my treatment," the woman snapped back. "You're being obtuse."

"And you're a liar. Either that or I'm seeing things. With all the prodding you did in my mind, I wouldn't be surprised."

Noah went rigid, the knowledge of Logan's pain making electricity spark through him again. Logan must have noticed, because he rocked Noah gently. "Shush. I'm fine. I'm here. We won't be apart again. Relax."

"*You* need to relax if you want him to do so," the woman told him. "And for the record, I do want to help."

Noah was very confused. Both Hugh and Logan obviously knew this person. She claimed to be able to cure him, but at the same time, she'd kidnapped Logan and had hurt Noah in the process. Noah needed some answers, and he needed them now. "Who are you?"

The woman smiled down at him. "I suppose I should introduce myself. My name is Anne Marie Hartman. I'm Raze's mother."

LOGAN HAD known Raze ever since they'd been children, and he remembered with crystal clarity the day Julian had been born. It was a little strange, because as it usually happened with childhood memories, a lot of things from that time had been forgotten, the details dulled by the years. But this, this remained clear, perhaps clearer than he'd have liked.

Raze had anticipated having a brother for months. Well, another brother, he'd said, because by then, he and Logan had been so close they considered each other siblings. He'd enthused over how much fun they'd have together. At one point, his enthusiasm had contaminated Logan, even if he was an only child and hadn't really wanted siblings beyond what Raze was to him.

And then Anne Marie Hartman had gone into labor, and suddenly Raze was left orphaned. Logan didn't know how they hadn't realized the pregnancy had been difficult, but even then, Lucius Hartman had been very protective of his son. Without a doubt, he'd hoped to shield Raze from the truth.

In the end, it hadn't helped, and Raze had been left with a scar of loss. His father had tried his best, but most of the time, he couldn't be around, needing to work extra hard so his two sons would lack for nothing. Then the virus had struck, and Lucius had fallen into a coma. Logan's own parents, who'd many times given Raze comfort, were killed. More pain, more death, more scars.

Seeing Anne Marie Hartman standing in front of him was like reliving all that. It should have been strange, because he'd come to terms with what had happened a long time ago. He and Uriel had become friends, even if it was painful for Logan to be in his presence. But Anne Marie had died in childbirth, before the virus. How could she be here, decades later?

"I know what you're thinking," she said, "that I should be dead. But I'm not, and further explanations can wait. Noah should be our focus now."

Questions burned through Logan, but he ignored them. As much as it irked him to agree with Anne Marie, she was right. Naturally, that didn't mean he had any intentions of allowing her to perform whatever insane treatment she'd come up with. "Hugh!" he called out. "Come here. We need help."

There was no answer and Logan looked over his shoulder, scanning the area. Hugh stood a few feet from him, trying to talk to a shell-shocked Julian. Logan's heart clenched. He was well aware Julian had always blamed himself for his mother's death. Unfortunately, that sort of thing always happened in cases of childbirth deaths. And with Raze and Lucius gone, Julian had been unstable. This information had undoubtedly hit him hard.

Anne Marie didn't seem to care. "You do realize neither of them truly wish for Noah's well-being. I'm sorry, Logan, but that's the truth. Hugh isn't capable of finding the cure, but even if he had been, he wouldn't have given it to you. He hates Uriel too much. He'd have killed Noah, but he's always been a good man, and his heart probably didn't allow it."

By now, even this conversation was too much for Noah. "They say Uriel is dead, Logan," he whispered, his eyes glassy. "But he isn't. I saw him. He was in the energy. We have to go back for him. We have to help him."

He tried to get up, but the movement made him wince in pain. Logan tried not to panic. This was even worse than before. At least the first time, Logan had the serum to fall back on. Whatever Hugh's faults, the substance had worked, and it kept Noah's cells stable. But he didn't have any medicine now. He was helpless. There was absolutely nothing he could do.

And Anne Marie knew it, damn her. She could have easily orchestrated this entire thing to put him in this horrible position. "He'll die," she told him. "He'll die if he doesn't undergo my treatment."

Logan bit his lip so hard it bled. "Can you really cure him?"

Anne Marie nodded. "Who do you think helped create him to begin with? I was the one to give the cloning technique to the purists. Of course, they managed to botch it even if they had the perfect DNA to work with, but that's beside the point."

Logan had no clue how to begin to address that, but when Noah curled against his chest, seeking his comfort, he realized there was another solution. "All right. We'll do things your way. But if you hurt him, you'll wish you *had* died in childbirth. It would have been less painful than what I plan to do to you."

"Then it's a good thing I don't plan on hurting him. Come. Follow me."

She got up, and Logan followed her example, carrying Noah in his arms. As they moved, Julian snapped out of his peculiar trance. "Wait! Is that true? Are you really my mother?"

A shadow of something painful passed over Anne Marie's face, but it disappeared so quickly Logan almost thought he'd imagined it. "I don't expect you to understand my reasons for leaving you. If you want to know more, come with us."

Julian's eyes filled with tears. "Just like that? You're leaving? After all this time, that's all I get?"

Anne Marie's face was a mask of stone. "Noah needs to undergo the treatment Hugh was incapable of providing. And while I'm aware he's an obstacle in the path of your romantic life, I'm afraid such considerations aren't a factor that can influence my plans and my duties. We need Noah. He's the only one who can stop what other people began."

Logan hated her then, hated her even more than he already did and hated that she was Noah's only hope. The look of complete and utter desolation in Julian's eyes struck him like a physical blow. But Logan had survived Raze's death with his sanity intact for one reason and one reason alone—the fact that Noah was still breathing. As much as he wanted to offer Julian comfort, he didn't have time now. And it hurt to know that his actions, like his presence, made things worse for Julian, that Julian would see it like yet another rejection. It was another choice, a painful one. There was only one thing he could do.

"Julian, this is a serious situation," he told his friend. "Noah could die, and this might be the only chance he has. I don't know what's going on any more than you do, and I don't trust her. But you need to hear what she has to say, if only for your own peace of mind."

The despair faded a little, or at least so Logan thought. Julian nodded, and Logan chose to deem that a sort of positive response. In his arms, Noah started to tremble, and Logan couldn't think about anything except him.

"He's getting worse," he said, wondering how in the world he'd come to rely on the woman who'd kidnapped him—and who turned out to be Raze's mother—to save the man he loved. "Do something."

"I'd love to," Anne Marie snapped at him. "Why do you think I wanted them to bring him to begin with?"

Behind them, Hugh released a soft bark of laughter. "Well, you're definitely not doing a very good job at being well-intentioned. You should have expected this when you took Logan."

"And I did, but he should have never been strong enough to use that kind of energy. Dammit."

The only good thing about the entire exchange was that Anne Marie seemed genuinely interested in helping Noah. As he ran after her, carrying his precious burden, Logan desperately hoped he was right about this, because otherwise, he'd lose Noah, and everything would be for naught.

Chapter Nine

AS SOON as he plopped into his hovercraft seat, Uriel leaned against Raze's shoulder, exhausted. "Well, that could have gone better."

They were returning from a meeting in northern Eden, where a group of cyborgs had hosted yet another revolt. They'd been trying so hard to do damage control, but it was nigh impossible to get through to these people. Uriel didn't blame them. They'd lost too much, and overnight, they'd found out the man they'd considered their only hope was the reason for that loss. Uriel wouldn't have taken it well either, but that didn't mean he had to like it.

Raze wrapped an arm around him, his warmth seeping into Uriel like a comforting balm. "It could have also been worse. And I'm so proud of you, baby. You're doing so well."

Some of the strain inside Uriel drained away. As hard as things had become, Uriel could always count on Raze. More than four years had passed since they'd met and fallen in love, and their relationship had never faltered. Sure, they had their arguments— what couple didn't?—but Raze had stood by his side through thick and thin. He was Uriel's rock at a time when nothing else was certain. Despite all the vitriol his own citizens shot at him, in Raze's embrace, Uriel felt safe.

He ended up dozing off a little, Raze still caressing his hair. The next thing he knew, Raze was shaking him awake.

"We're here, baby. Home sweet home."

123

These days, Genesis was anything but sweet. Even so, Uriel couldn't help a small smile. "I think this weekend we should take some time for ourselves. We deserve it."

"That sounds like heaven," Raze told him as Uriel got up. "I've forgotten when we last did that. Just... stopped."

Uriel knew exactly what Raze meant. Between their international trips and their attempts to reassure their people, they were forced to move too fast to actually enjoy each other's presence. Sometimes it felt like Uriel saw Noah more—and Noah was still in cryo.

As they left the hovercraft, Uriel thought back to a happier time, when he and Noah had been together, when he and Raze had shared hope they could rebuild Eden, make it stronger, better. That hope was a distant dream now, and Uriel might have cried at the loss of it if he hadn't still clung to Raze.

He must have fallen silent, because Raze stopped before they could exit the hangars. "Hey. I know things are pretty awful, but you need to have faith. The worst is over."

"I suppose you're right." Uriel sighed. "It was too big of a secret to be kept buried forever. I just hate... I don't want to be a virus, Raze."

"Too late for that," a woman's voice said from behind him.

Uriel tried to turn, intending to face their unexpected companion. He only managed to do it halfway, the move aborted when Raze forcibly shoved him down. He registered the distinctive sound of a phaser going off, and then he hit the floor, Raze on top of him.

He wasn't exactly unused to people shooting at him. In fact, he'd been the target of countless death threats, and during their trip to Iberia, there had been more than one unintelligent terrorist who'd tried to bypass his security, only to be thwarted by a furious, protective Raze. Uriel had reached a point where he wasn't worried about himself, only about his lover.

As much faith as he had in Raze's skills, that hadn't changed, and as soon as he caught his breath, he rolled over and checked Raze's condition. He should have probably focused on taking out the person who'd targeted them, but he was afraid, so very afraid.

His dread turned out to be justified, because Raze didn't move. His face was slack, body motionless. For a few dreadful moments, Uriel thought Raze was dead, but no, he was still breathing... barely.

His own breath staggering, Uriel shook his lover. "Raze. Come on, Raze. Open your eyes. Look at me."

Raze still didn't come to. He didn't move. Terror buried its claws deep in Uriel's heart, so intense it choked him. He couldn't get enough air, the fear cloying, viscous, invading his lungs like a physical thing.

Footsteps approached, and the woman's voice returned. "This is your fault," she said, a slight tremor hinting at her agitation. "Your fault. For everything."

Uriel looked up and in the daze of his anger, he managed to recognize Odette, one of Raze's friends and fellow soldiers. The knowledge barely computed, because she didn't get a second chance to hit him. She crumpled to the floor like a puppet with her strings cut, her body twitching as Uriel's power coursed through her.

That didn't help Uriel much when it came to Raze, but thankfully, the rest of the cyborgs in their home must have been alerted that something was wrong. Raze's father burst into the hangars, followed by three other men. As the guards gathered around Odette, Lucius dropped to his knees next to Raze and checked Raze's pulse. The frown on his face spoke volumes of the seriousness of the situation.

"We need to get him some medical attention, stat. Uriel, you have to move."

It was only then that Uriel realized he was holding on to Raze so tightly Lucius couldn't approach out of fear he would bear the brunt of Uriel's pain. Uriel nodded, although the words were coming to him through a haze of panic, guilt, and anger. He forced himself to let go and allowed Lucius to pick up Raze. The older cyborg rushed toward the medical bay with Uriel trailing closely behind him.

Lucius's physician of choice, Hugh Wells, wasn't there today. He spent a lot of time at Noah's facility, still trying to come up with a cure. Or at least that was the official reason both he and Raze's brother, Julian, had given. Sometimes Uriel thought they just didn't want to stay in Genesis because they didn't want to see him.

Not that it mattered this time around. Even Hugh's considerable talents would have been useless. Uriel held his breath throughout the countless scans and checkups, but never once did Raze stir. And when Lucius approached him, Uriel couldn't say he was surprised at the cyborg's words.

"The phaser was set to kill. Because Raze pushed you down, the energy bolt hit him in the forehead. His mental computer short-circuited. We've done scans for any sign of brain activity, but we haven't found any."

Uriel didn't reply. He'd already realized it, figured out the angle of the hit and the effect it was likely to have on Raze. The energy blast hadn't left any outward physical traces, but the internal injuries rendered Raze beyond aid, or at least, whatever aid the doctors could provide.

Uriel had already decided on a course of action. He approached Raze's cyber tube and set his hand on the glass, staring at the handsome face he knew so well. Inside the machine, Raze almost looked like he was just sleeping, but Uriel saw past that. Raze had been so vibrant, so full of life and passion. He would never be so still, not even in slumber.

"It's okay, Raze," he whispered. "I'll fix it."

He had rebooted Raze's implants before. He could do it again. Not to mention that since then, he'd helped countless other cyborgs, including Raze's father, and ironically, Odette.

It was Lucius who tried to stop Uriel from going through with his plan. The old cyborg set his hand on Uriel's shoulder and squeezed it tightly. "Uriel, I know you want to help him. I want you to do it just as much. But...." Lucius swallowed, as if he couldn't quite bring himself to finish the phrase. "But you have to keep in mind the effects of your power. It's risky."

"I'm not afraid," Uriel replied automatically. "I can do it. I know I can."

"We're talking about a brain injury," Lucius protested. "Even if you do fix the mental computer, there's no guarantee Raze will recover. And the effects on you could be devastating."

"I realize that, Lucius," Uriel answered, touched. It meant a lot that Lucius showed such concern for Uriel when Raze's life was at risk. "But Raze is everything to me. I have to believe he can come back."

Lucius sighed heavily. "It won't be easy."

Uriel almost laughed. When had things ever been easy for him? His life had always been littered with burdens he had accepted as natural. Raze's love had changed all that, and he refused to lose it. They'd already lost too much. Besides, if anyone could help Raze, it was Uriel. He had felt Raze's implants before, and he knew just how important Raze's mental computer was. If he managed to reboot it, the cyber tube would be able to fix the rest of the organic damage.

"Step away," he told Lucius. "I'm doing it."

Lucius didn't try to stop him again. He left the room, although Uriel suspected the cyborg didn't go very far. It didn't matter. Uriel focused on Raze, on how much he wanted his lover back. He could do this. He had to.

Lucius had been right to warn him, though. As he sought out Raze's injury, pain erupted over him. It was far more intense than anything he'd ever experienced in his life. Uriel almost recoiled, but he kept going. He kept going even when something inside him screamed to stop. He couldn't stop, not until Raze was back with him.

But no matter how strong his resolve, Uriel couldn't control everything. His mind exploded with confusing images, memories of the past mingling with fears for the future. Clouded figures danced just within his view—Raze, Noah, even his dead mother he tried not to think about. She had warned him, and she'd been right, because his secret, the secret of his birth, had killed Raze.

No, Uriel couldn't believe that. He refused to give up. The price he had to pay might be steep, but Raze was more important than him, than anything. So Uriel gave and gave until something inside him snapped, and he couldn't stop giving, couldn't stop screaming, simply couldn't stop. And it hurt, it hurt so much, and all Uriel could think was no no no no. He'd failed Raze so badly.

The world drifted into a confusing limbo, and then he was opening his eyes in a panic. He nearly screamed when he realized he was in a tube of sorts and water surrounded him, threatening to swallow him whole. Hell, he couldn't vocalize the shout in his throat since his mouth was covered with some sort of device. Similarly, he couldn't break the tube, because his hands and legs were secured in restraints.

He had no idea how he'd gotten here. The tube seemed to be encroaching on his consciousness, hammering out his sense of self, and he was so afraid, impossibly afraid because he couldn't see Raze, couldn't touch him, couldn't even call out to him, and Raze had been dead.

Oh, no, dead.

Power crackled within him, and he lashed out at the tech holding him captive. Even if he was in the water, the bioenergy didn't recoil against him, but then he had known that would be the case. A side effect of his power was that he managed to absorb regular energy without getting hurt. It was so stupid. If Raze hadn't pushed him down, he would have most likely survived the phaser shot. But Raze…. No, Raze….

He tried to focus, tried to force the tube open, but he couldn't quite get a grip anymore. He might have physically tried to break free, but he didn't have to. The water started to drain out. The device covering his mouth retreated, and the glass slid aside as the tube opened. He staggered out dazed and uncertain, and he would have fallen if he hadn't landed in a familiar, protective embrace instead.

"Shh. It's okay, baby. You're safe. I'm here."

The voice reached out to him, cutting through his train of thought with the precision of a laser scalpel. Logan. Logan was here, holding him, real and alive. The world swirled and tilted, and then Noah blinked and stared up at his lover.

"What… what happened?"

Logan cupped his cheek, and his fingers shook slightly. "You felt ill after using your power. We brought you in for medical attention. You don't remember?"

Oh, Noah remembered. He remembered everything—Julian, Hugh, the strange vortex, Logan's kidnapping, Raze's mother, and then... Raze and Uriel.

He started to tremble as Uriel's pain echoed inside him again, and Logan tightened his hold on him. "It's okay. You don't have to strain yourself. Just relax. You're all right. Everything is going to be all right."

Logan whispered countless reassurances in his ear. At one point, the words blended together until Noah couldn't even understand them. Still, the sound of Logan's voice anchored Noah, and soon the fear and the darkness encroaching on his vision drifted away.

"I saw Uriel," he managed to explain. Then he realized that didn't sound right and shook his head. "I felt him. I *was* him. I... he was trying to save Raze."

Logan's eyes widened. "You... were him?"

Noah nodded. "It's happened before, but only in the memories we shared. This time it was different. I could feel his pain over losing me." When he'd come to, he hadn't been Noah at all, and only Logan's presence had snapped him out of it.

"How is that possible?" Logan turned to look at someone behind him. "You said the treatment wouldn't hurt him. This isn't my idea of not hurt."

"Well, Logan, I can't say I expected it," a woman answered, "but I can tell you it isn't the treatment that caused it."

Noah freed himself from Logan's embrace and stole a look at her, at Raze's mother. His hackles rose when he met her gaze. "What are you doing here? What do you want with us?"

She arched a brow. "Do you even know where 'here' is?"

Actually, Noah hadn't gotten a good look around, since the damn tube had short-circuited his complex thought processes. Now that he did, he realized she had a point. He didn't have a clue as to his current location.

The last thing he remembered, he'd used his power to take out the mercs attacking Logan. After that, his condition had struck back, and his memories grew fuzzy from there, until they coalesced into Uriel's.

He didn't want to display any fear, but he took a step back, retreating into Logan's embrace. She wasn't the one who scared him, just this uncertainty, never knowing what he should do. His destiny had been written for him when the purists had brought him into being as a clone. The fragility of his body kept him from rushing to his brother's aid, just like it had forced him into cryo and away from the man he loved.

"Back off," Logan snapped at Raze's mother. "You're not helping."

"Fair enough." She sighed. "Look, Noah, I know you don't trust me. Logan doesn't trust me either, but you were very sick, and I was the only one who could give you the care you needed. So we brought you here, and I managed to administer the treatment in time. You'll have to tell me if there are any side effects, although as far as we can tell, it worked."

Noah didn't know what she meant until he caught a glimpse of his own reflection in the glass of a nearby cyber tube. He looked just like he had before he'd started decomposing. There were no lines, no gray hairs, none of the things he'd tried so hard to ignore when he'd come back. His hair was long again, which made Noah wonder how long the treatment had lasted.

"You were out for a week," Logan said, as if guessing his thoughts. "I was so afraid that I'd made a mistake in trusting her with you."

Raze's mother—Anne Marie, if Noah's memory served—scoffed. "If I'd wanted to hurt him, I would have just held back on the treatment. And I know you feared I would attack his mind, but that's impossible on a clone. Noah's mind is crowded as it is."

"Crowded?" Noah repeated.

"You said it yourself. You were Uriel. Admittedly, I didn't expect quite this level of connection, but I had hoped for it."

Noah was getting exasperated. He didn't understand anything anymore. It befuddled him how Raze's supposedly dead mother could be the one to help him when Hugh Wells had failed. The dynamics of the entire situation boggled the mind, and Noah was sick and tired of losing, fearing, and hurting, all because of the machinations of others.

130

This time when he took a step forward, he did so with renewed determination. He summoned his bioenergy without fear, testing Anne Marie's claims and his ability to take back the reins of his life.

It was strange, but in the past he hadn't realized the burden he placed on himself when using his bioenergy. Uriel had said there was always a price to be paid, especially when they had to fix implants, so Noah had deemed his own experience normal. But now he felt different, like the power buzzing through his cells truly belonged to him. It had always been an extension of his will, but now he sensed it with a far greater clarity.

He realized then that he could do this, could finally embrace his power without risking death. He allowed sparks to dance over his fingers as he fixed Anne Marie with a glare.

"You hoped for it. You hoped for and did many things. How could you? How could you abandon your children and your husband?" Anger rushed over him as he spoke. "How could you hurt Logan? With everything that you did, what can you possibly expect from me?"

She faced him without flinching even if she couldn't have missed his threatening demeanor. "I have no reason to explain my choices to you, at least not when it comes to my family. Logan... I don't like that I had to involve him, or Julian for that matter, but there was no other way. I needed to find you before it was too late."

"Too late for what?" Noah asked.

He already knew the answer before she replied. "Uriel. It's getting worse, and you're the only one who can stop it, Noah. You have a strong bond with Uriel. It's confirmed. His consciousness reached out to you while you were undergoing my treatment. You can go to Genesis and fix it."

Noah should have been wary of anything she suggested. He didn't trust her in the slightest. However, he trusted his heart, and ever since he'd seen Uriel's figure within the vortex, he'd wanted to go to his brother.

Logan wasn't so easily persuaded. He kept a tight hold on Noah and fixed Anne Marie with a frustrated glare. "I thought we'd already established the bioenergy would harm him."

"That was before," she replied. "His cells are stable now."

"Somehow I'm not reassured," Logan snapped at her. "How is he even supposed to stop Uriel?"

Anne Marie gave him a telling look, but Noah ignored her. "I can reach out to him, Logan. I know I can. He's my brother. Once I'm there, I'll know what I have to do."

"Noah, that's too risky. You don't know what Uriel's power will do to you. No one who was trapped inside ever came out—purist or cyborg, and I can't lose you."

Logan's concern meant the world to Noah. It had been the one constant in his life, throughout the entire existence he could call his. Logan had been the first one to reach out to him, and that hadn't changed. So Noah was actually reassured. In fact, he felt better and more decided than he had in a long time.

Perhaps Anne Marie's treatment had truly worked. For once, his body wasn't screaming in protest, wasn't trying to sabotage what he had with Logan. If that also meant he could help Uriel, Noah couldn't have been more grateful for it.

Gripping Logan's chin, he forced his lover to face him. "Uriel needs me. I heard him. I felt his pain. I have to go to him. And I know what you're going to say, but I won't hurt him, and he won't hurt me."

"But—"

"Don't worry." Noah interrupted Logan before he could finish. "We've already been apart for too long. I'll come back to you. I promise you that."

Logan looked like he wanted to protest, but in the end he didn't. His frown settled into a resigned yet loving smile. "And I'll be waiting."

The words reminded Noah of all the time Logan had spent waiting. Five years alone, five years they'd never get back. That knowledge solidified Noah's decision. He'd fix this. He could do it. Because he wasn't just a clone, a worthless copy. He was Noah, Uriel's brother and Logan's lover.

"Take me to Genesis," he told Raze's mother. "It's high time we ended this."

She scowled. "This isn't exactly what I had in mind. You need a weapon. There's only one way the vortex will fade and that's—"

"No!" Noah cut her off. "I don't believe that. Uriel is still in there, and I can bring him back. I won't hurt him. He's been through enough."

"You're willing to chance all of our lives, including Logan's, based on the dim hope that there's still something of your brother out there?" She gave him a look of disbelief. "You can't be serious. I didn't push you through such a difficult treatment for this."

Noah hesitated. If there was someone he loved more than Uriel, it was Logan, and she knew it, damn her. Logan wrapped an arm around his shoulder and held him close. "Ignore her. Don't think about us for now. Think about what you need to do, and what you think is right."

"If I don't try to help him, I'll never forgive myself," Noah whispered.

Logan nodded. "I understand. I would have done the same for Raze, if I'd been given the chance."

His words seemed to hit something inside Anne Marie, because she didn't hesitate further. She guided him and Logan out of the strange lab, into a winding corridor. Noah didn't see anyone else, and he distantly wondered what had happened to Hugh and Julian. He wondered where he was in the first place. He didn't get the chance to ask, because Anne Marie finally opened a door and nudged him inside. "You can wash and rest a bit here. There are also clean clothes. When you're ready, I'll be waiting for you."

She left them standing there, in the doorway of the strange, unfamiliar room. For a few moments, they just stared at each other, speechless. And it wasn't that Noah didn't know what to say. They'd already spoken a lot when Anne Marie had been with them. But for some reason, it was different now, when they were in private.

He couldn't be sure who reached for whom first, but the next thing he knew, he was in Logan's arms, with Logan kissing him. It wasn't a deep kiss, but rather an avalanche of small ones, peppered all over his face, his lips, his eyelids, every inch of him Logan could reach with his mouth from this position. It was as if Logan didn't have enough patience to linger on a kiss, and Noah completely understood.

He pushed Logan into the room without letting go of his shirt. In fact, he managed the extraordinary feat of closing the door without even glancing at it or moving his hands off Logan. He was afraid, afraid that if he let go of Logan now, they'd be separated again. And he knew it would happen. He knew he needed to go find his brother, and every second he indulged in Logan's kisses was one more second of pain for Uriel. But he still couldn't bring himself to break the embrace, not yet.

"I missed you so much," Logan murmured. "So much."

Noah wanted to say that too, but truth be told, he hadn't been the one to suffer most because of their separation. He'd slept for the better part of it, while Logan had been forced to endure it alone, not even knowing if Noah would ever wake.

It might have been hard for Noah to withstand the tubes he'd been forced into for the treatment, but it hurt even more to acknowledge the pain Logan must have gone through. And it didn't help that it wasn't over yet.

They kissed frantically for a while longer. It wasn't even about carnal pleasure, not really. Noah might only be wearing the jumpsuit provided by Raze's mother for the purpose of the treatment, but even if the garment did next to nothing to hide his body, neither of them was truly seeking anything sexual.

In a way, Noah wanted it, the sensuality. He'd always wanted Logan, even at a time when he had tried to hide it from himself and everyone else. But their relationship and their closeness went beyond sex, and when they collapsed together on the couch, they didn't take things further. Noah would have liked a proper reunion, to have Logan physically claim him as his, but at the same time, he didn't think it would feel right, not now, not with everything looming ahead, so many burdens and so much pain.

When they broke apart, the look in Logan's eyes crushed Noah. It practically screamed "Don't go" even if Logan didn't speak. Noah loved him for not saying it because it would have made things harder. He loved Logan for understanding, even if it forced them into yet another separation.

As if guessing his thoughts, Logan smiled. "I believe in you, baby. You can do this. I wish you didn't have to, but I believe you can do it."

That meant more to Noah than he could ever say, and it gave him the strength to do what needed to be done. "Thank you," he whispered as he got up.

Unexpectedly, Logan grabbed his arm. "Wait. There's something you need to know."

Noah's stomach flipped as he wondered what other ill news he could receive. Had something more happened while he'd been unconscious? At this point, nothing seemed out of the realm of possibility. "What is it?" he asked, hating the way his voice trembled.

"I.... When I went after Abraham Zion, I found some unexpected files about a hidden project. Project... Regenesis. Does that sound...."

Noah didn't hear anything else after that. He saw Logan's mouth move, but the actual words.... No, they didn't fit what echoed in his ears, in his mind.

Suddenly, he remembered everything. The tank, the same one that had haunted him from the moment he'd first come to be. Abigail and Ezekiel, standing there next to it, idly planning yet another virus. Enslavement. *With Project Regenesis, the world will be ours.*

They had not realized he could hear them. Whenever they'd needed to gloat, they'd come there, hashing out the details of their plan. He'd registered it all. It came so clearly to him now, through the haze of the nightmares and the guilt that had plagued him, through the confusion, the fear, and the self-loathing. He had known it all along.

A single tear slid down his cheek. Was he relieved that he finally knew why he'd killed them? Yes, he was. It didn't change his guilt, and didn't wash the blood off his hands, but it helped him gain new perspective. Because if he hadn't acted the way he had, Logan would most likely be lost to him. Just the idea scared him more than the container he'd been trapped in.

Logan brushed his fingers over Noah's cheeks, wiping his tears, and Noah finally managed to focus on his lover. Logan smiled at him. "See? I told you you're not a killer."

Noah still couldn't quite believe that, but he believed he'd done what he'd been forced to do given the circumstances. Maybe he'd never been as worthless as he'd thought. Maybe Logan had been right all along. And if that was the case, it was all the more important to go to Uriel's rescue.

He had no words that would express everything he felt. Instead, he allowed himself a few more moments to process what he'd learned, taking comfort in Logan's familiar scent. When he couldn't stall any longer, he broke away from Logan and headed into the bathroom.

He washed quickly and expediently, then dressed in the provided clothes, which, as it turned out, were very similar to what he'd worn before. Logan gave him privacy for it. Although a small part of Noah wished his lover had followed him into the bathroom, he knew they couldn't afford the delay.

Finally he was ready, or as ready as he was going to get. It helped that Logan wrapped an arm around his shoulders the moment he stepped out of the bathroom. Even so, Noah remained more aware than ever that he'd have to do this alone, that Logan couldn't follow him into the vortex. In a way, it was a relief, because no matter how afraid he might be, he didn't want Logan at risk.

By the time they reunited with Raze and Julian's mother, Noah had managed to calm down. Anne Marie didn't comment on his demeanor. Perhaps she'd expected it. Either way, she led him—and Logan, who refused to leave his side—to a hovercraft. With quick, efficient movements, she activated the controls, and once they were all secure in their seats, they were off.

At first, the hovercraft flew too fast for him to get a good idea of where they'd been, but Noah guessed it when he caught sight of the city in the distance. Noah hadn't gotten the chance to explore Eden too much, and neither had Uriel, but he was familiar with the sight of Zion. Anne Marie had built her facility a good distance away from the actual settlement, but taking into account how long they'd traveled, he had a pretty good idea of his previous location.

As they traveled, Logan gave him more details on the situation. "We tried everything to get a read of the vortex and push it back, but no tech works. Here's what little data we managed to acquire."

He brought up a few files on the hovercraft side screens, and Noah scanned them carefully. None of it came as a surprise, since Noah had seen the vortex with his own eyes. Still, the information hammered one point home. Noah was the last option they had at their disposal. In all likelihood, this was the reason why Logan had even agreed to him going.

The seriousness of the situation was further revealed when they reached their destination. Just like Anne Marie had told him, the vortex had grown. It had engulfed not only the cryo freeze facility Noah had once lived in, but a far larger area beyond it. In fact, it was rapidly heading toward Zion.

When Anne Marie stopped her hovercraft two miles away from the whirlpool of energy, Noah thought the distance was too great, impractical given the urgency of their situation. But as he slid out of his seat, he noticed that with every passing second, the vortex approached more and more. In mere minutes, it would be dangerously close.

"We don't have much time," she said, obviously knowing this as well. "I wish I could give you advice, but I have no idea what you'll find in there. The only thing I know is that this is Uriel's energy you will face. Your body is no longer unstable at a cellular level. I made sure of that. So you should be immune to the vortex. But... I can't tell you anything else."

He heard the disapproval in her voice and knew she still didn't agree with his approach. He had some questions of his own, and he wished he had the time to find out how and why she'd come to be here and have such knowledge. But he didn't, so he nodded and turned toward Logan. "Remember what I said. I'll come back to you."

This time Logan didn't answer. Instead, he pulled Noah close and crushed their mouths together. Unlike before, the kiss was devastating, feeding the flame of desire inside Noah, a desire he couldn't yet address. But oh, he wanted to, how he wanted to. He wrapped his arms around Logan's neck, drinking in Logan's taste as reassurance and encouragement. A selfish part of him never wanted to let go, would have preferred to stay in Logan's arms. At some level, he wished he and Logan had stayed in that room, just the two of them, forever. But they had lost a lot within the vortex, and it was up to Noah to get it back. Until then, he didn't have the right to surrender to his own selfish desires.

He broke away from Logan, reluctance and love mixing inside him, warring with his affection and duty as a brother. He wished he didn't have to go, but saying so outright would be cruel.

"Love you," he whispered instead against Logan's lips.

Logan let him go then, although his torn, lost look made Noah waver. It was Anne Marie who snapped him out of his trance. "I'm afraid the vortex is coming closer. It's dangerous for us to stay here. We'll monitor it from back at the base."

Noah got the message. He stole one last look at Logan, and then leaped out of the hovercraft. As he stepped back, Anne Marie already pored over the controls. Noah waited in the same spot, watching while she started the vehicle. To be fair, he wasn't really seeing much of her, too focused on Logan to care about much else.

The hovercraft took off and sped away into the distance, and Noah was alone. He turned toward the approaching vortex and within it, he thought he saw his brother reaching out to him. Taking a deep breath, he walked forward, wary, but at the same time excited.

All of a sudden, the bright light rushed toward him. Noah froze in his tracks, but he didn't have time to retreat, even if he had planned on fleeing. Before he could process what was happening, the vortex swallowed him whole.

He didn't know what he'd been expecting, but it certainly wasn't... nothing. Well, that wasn't quite accurate. The sight that spread out in front of Noah couldn't honestly be described as nothingness. Rather it was Eden, the Eden he knew from Uriel's memories and his own.

Some things had changed, but Noah guessed most of the differences were the natural result of the passage of time. He recognized the verdant plains of the Zion Plateau, and it didn't slip his notice that the once prosperous fields were largely lying fallow. That could be because the effect of the vortex had kept Edenians from tending to them, but somehow, Noah doubted that was the case.

When Noah had gone into cryo, Uriel had been planning to expand the agriculture of Eden, to include more of the tech the purist regime had often spurned. Industry had also been a target, its overhaul necessary since it had been largely based on cyborg abuse. The possible war with Iberia had changed priorities. Even so, throughout all this, Zion had remained one of the most important cities in Eden, a supply point vital to Genesis's well-being.

God only knew what had happened once Zion's governor had turned against Uriel. Judging by the state of the fields, Noah guessed a lot of people must have taken up arms against his brother.

When he fully processed the thought, he realized he might be leaping to conclusions. Fallow fields didn't necessarily mean war or revolt. Even under the circumstances, their existence could have been caused by a million other things.

And yet, Noah knew his first guess had been right. Light danced all around him, the source of the information infusing his pores with purpose and familiarity. Noah stared out into the distance, at the road he knew led toward Genesis. Even if it was still daytime, stars seemed to glitter above him. A whisper of a voice sounded in his ear.

Noah didn't turn. He knew he wouldn't find anyone there. Instead, he steeled himself for the long trip and started walking.

"I SHOULDN'T have let him go. I should have stayed with him. This is going to end in disaster."

As soon as Logan lost sight of Noah, he began having doubts. Well, the doubts had already been there, but he'd trusted Noah enough to squash them. Now his panic over Noah's absence was taking over. Noah's condition seemed to have improved after Anne Marie's treatment, but the knowledge that his life depended on her truthfulness weighed heavily on Logan.

He'd been so desperate when he'd agreed to her plan, realizing Noah was slipping away, his cells disintegrating, unstable. When Noah had come out of the tube, he'd looked like himself again. But he'd also been frightened, and according to Noah himself, Uriel.

Logan stole another look toward the vortex and set his jaw. "Stop the hovercraft. I'm getting out."

Anne Marie threw a gaze over her shoulder, arching a brow. "You do realize there's nothing you can do to help him. This is something only Noah can handle."

"Whatever the case, I'm not going any farther. I want to stick as close to him as I can." His body and soul were screaming with that need, so much so that he could barely breathe.

"Fair enough," Anne Marie said. "If things go according to plan, staying here won't be all that dangerous." She released a soft, bitter laugh. "Then again, if it doesn't work, running won't help anyone."

She'd explained her theory before. According to her, Uriel's bioenergy would eventually expand to engulf the whole of Eden. She claimed that, given time, it might even cross the ocean and hit other continents.

Logan would have thought that was a little much, but hell, twenty-five years ago, he wouldn't have believed a genetically engineered person could be turned into a virus that would short-circuit implants of cyborgs all over the world. Furthermore, if anyone had told him he'd fall in love with the clone of that virus, he'd have likely deemed them insane.

So Logan no longer considered anything beyond the realm of possibility. He took things one day at a time and did whatever he could with the choices he had at any given moment. Right now, he had two options: stay or go. His course of action was clear.

Anne Marie didn't try to dissuade him again. She directed the hovercraft toward Zion. Once they reached the outskirts of the city, she stopped the aircraft, at which point Logan got out.

"Keep monitoring the vortex," he told her, "and for fuck's sake, talk to Julian. You can't delay it forever."

She didn't answer, not that Logan expected her to. She'd refused to provide any sort of explanation regarding her sudden return from the dead, and while Hugh and Julian were both staying at her facility, she had yet to approach her son for a long overdue conversation. Not for the first time, Logan wondered what Raze would have done if he'd been alive, and the pang of distress he felt at the thought accompanied him even as he watched Anne Marie's hovercraft take off once more, then disappear into the distance.

He didn't linger too much on the thought, knowing there was nothing he could do about it. Instead, he turned on his heel and headed into the abandoned city.

Unsurprisingly, Zion was a ghost town. It was strange to remember that a few months back, when the truth about Project Uriel had come out, Zion had stood as the center of opposition against Uriel. Logan had been here then, part of the forces dispatched to ensure order. It was probably the most frustrating mission he'd ever had, since he couldn't even trust his own men to watch his back.

In the end, it was Uriel himself who'd ended the revolt, with a show of force Logan knew had cost him. He hadn't wanted to harm his own people, but when he'd come to try to reason with them, they'd attacked him and Raze, and it had kind of turned out that way. One would have thought people had learned from that mistake, but apparently they hadn't, since the same thing had happened in Genesis.

No Edenians had actually died the day of the revolt, but they'd all left after it had become obvious the vortex would soon swallow their city. Homes, vehicles, stores—everything was abandoned. It was truly disheartening to see how such a great city had fallen so low. Worse, Logan didn't have anyone to blame—well, no one alive. The purist Council members were dead, and that was yet another thing Logan didn't want to think about, if only because he should have realized sooner what their deaths meant for all of them, and for Noah specifically.

Shaking himself, Logan headed out into the city. The first thing he needed to do was to find a vehicle of his own. Even if he couldn't venture closer to the vortex right now, he had a feeling Noah would need him, and soon.

Chapter Ten

NOAH HAD feared he'd have to travel to Genesis on foot. He wasn't afraid of physical effort, but the time it would have taken for him to do that seemed impractical at best, and ridiculous in all fairness. Fortunately, luck was with him, and he found an abandoned hovercraft after an hour or so of trekking through the fields.

In truth, it wasn't actually abandoned. There were people inside, two men of about Raze's age. They must have been trying to escape the vortex, but had failed, because they now lay motionless in the vehicle that should have helped them.

Noah had a moment during which he hesitated sliding into the aircraft. There was something… not right about taking it. Or maybe it just felt off to fly the damn thing all the way to Genesis with two dead cyborgs still inside. No, in all likelihood, what he hated was the confirmation of what Uriel had done. It might not have been on purpose, but Uriel would never see it that way. If he was still alive and Noah managed to reach out to his consciousness, Uriel would never forgive himself for it.

For that reason, Noah almost staggered with relief when he realized the cyborgs were still breathing. He had no idea how that was possible, but then again, taking into account the fast advance of the vortex, the cyborgs must have been hit by it earlier today, or within the last twelve hours at least.

He debated going back and trying to track down help or taking the two to Zion before realizing it would be far too time-consuming.

Anne Marie had said she and Logan would monitor the situation, but if Noah didn't come to Uriel's aid, the vortex would continue to grow, and any location he found for the injured men would stop being safe.

Murmuring an apology, Noah slid inside the pilot's seat and swept his fingers over the controls. He didn't even have to summon his bioenergy. The hovercraft started so quickly Noah barely had time to brace himself for it. He grabbed the armrest of his seat, somehow managing to avoid stumbling forward into the panel.

"Sorry about that," a familiar voice said as Noah secured the safety belt around his waist.

Noah went rigid and looked up at the panels, only to meet Uriel's eyes from the vidscreen. The image didn't display any location Noah could recognize, but it was definitely Uriel.

"Uriel.... Oh, God, I was so worried about you."

Uriel shot him a tired smile. "I wish I could tell you there's nothing to worry about, but as you can see, that's not the case."

Noah was more aware than ever of the two unconscious men in the hovercraft. Other cyborgs had been inside the vortex for months. Even if the energy itself hadn't killed them, without sustenance of any kind they would have slowly wasted away by now.

"Uriel—"

"I need you to stop me, Noah," his brother said, cutting him off. "I.... There are so many things... I can't...."

The transmission cut off, and Uriel's image dissipated into individual pixels. The hovercraft staggered and would have probably crashed if Noah hadn't set his hands on the console and used his power to take control.

So Uriel was aware of what he was doing, but he couldn't stop it. Was Uriel's mind free of his body? Was that what had happened after Uriel had tried to fix Raze's mental computer?

It made sense. If Uriel had suffered severe brain damage in the attempt to bring his lover back, his power could have rushed out of control. And Uriel's tone in those handful of phrases he'd spoken to Noah.... There was so much heartbreak, confusion, and loss.

144

Dammit. What was he going to do? He didn't have a plan beyond trying to speak with his brother.

Maybe that had been foolish. Maybe Anne Marie had been right when she'd tried to tell him to bring a weapon along. But no, he refused to dwell on that horrible thought. There had to be another way, another method that would allow him to bring his brother back.

For fuck's sake, he was a clone, and he'd managed to regain control of his body with the help of the supposedly dead mother of his brother's lover. Said lover had a brother of his own, who was in turn infatuated with Noah's other half. In a world where so few things made sense, the weirdness of it all provided hope, the hope that there might be something in Genesis, the miracle he needed to fix what was broken.

The trip lasted far too long for his comfort, and it tired him while also confirming he was in far better medical condition than he'd been before. He used his abilities liberally to control the hovercraft, but when Genesis loomed ahead, he wasn't in any pain.

He hadn't run into any more hovercrafts, and Noah guessed the vortex had just recently started to grow at such an accelerated pace and must have taken the two men with him by surprise. Once he reached Genesis, though, it was obvious that the capital had been hit just as suddenly, and far harder. He couldn't see any unconscious people, which should have been a good thing, but also scared him. What actually struck him was the silence. Genesis seemed to have been frozen in time, or floating in a peculiar limbo. The only thing that anchored Noah in reality was the buzz of the energy over his skin. It felt strange, familiar, yet not. It reminded him of the countless times he'd spent hours by his brother's side, talking, learning, coming up with ideas to improve Eden or just enjoying each other's presence, sometimes just the two of them, more often with Raze and Logan around. That warmth Noah remembered seemed tainted with something ominous now, and he knew he needed to hurry.

He directed the hovercraft toward the mansion, his heart beating faster and faster the closer he got. And then, all of a sudden, he lost control of the aircraft.

That was another thing he had not expected. Throughout the past hours, he'd gotten used to the vehicle working exactly as he told it to, but something felt different here. Maybe it wasn't the hovercraft that posed the problem, but Noah himself.

The familiar energy that had given Noah comfort lashed out against him, or rather, within him. Noah felt it try to worm its way into him, pushing at the boundaries of his consciousness. Images and feelings swamped him, and the hovercraft crashed into a nearby building as Noah struggled to push it all back.

His skin crawled, and every inch of his body screamed in protest. He staggered out of the hovercraft, dazed, wanting nothing more than to run, to retreat back to Logan's arms and safety. But his legs wouldn't obey and instead of retreating, he walked forward, heading deeper into the light, continuing his journey to the one home he'd ever known.

He ended up stumbling, falling to his knees right there in the middle of the street. Uriel's voice sounded in his ear. "Please, Noah. Please, help me."

"I want to," Noah replied. "Why won't you let me?"

No reply came. Instead, the strange energy rushed into Noah again, and it scared him like his brother never had before.

He'd always been acutely aware that Uriel was more powerful than him. He'd deemed it fitting, since he was only a copy, and copies were never quite as good as the real thing. Even his so-called mother had realized it toward the end. But he'd never begrudged Uriel for it, and had never thought a day would come when he'd have to stand against his brother.

But it had come, because this was without a doubt Uriel. Noah couldn't understand what his brother thought he was doing, but he knew he could not allow it.

Help me, the voice said again, this time inside Noah's mind. It latched onto Noah almost brutally, and Noah tasted fear in his mouth, a fear both his own and not. Uriel's fear.

It was acrid, terror, guilt, and agony spreading through him like a poison. Noah almost lost it at first, almost succumbed to it.

Oddly, it was the memory of his similar experiences that kept him from doing so.

He'd forgotten the number of times he'd woken from nightmares that taunted him with the inability to stop the bloodshed, nightmares with causes he hadn't even fully understood. At one point, only one thing had kept him going, or rather, one man. Logan.

Uriel had an anchor too, a man who protected him from himself. It made sense really. Both of them had been experiments, and their power was far too dangerous for lone individuals to control without support.

Hell, Uriel hadn't managed to tap into his own potential until he'd met Raze. It stood to reason that losing Raze unhinged his brother.

And it hurt, because Noah understood how that felt, at least to some extent. Logan's kidnapping had put him in a similar state of mind, and the need to rescue his lover had prevented disaster. Obviously Uriel hadn't been as lucky as him.

His empathy toward Uriel's plight made him feel Uriel's pain all the more acutely, but he summoned his memories of Logan to keep the energy at bay. *Please,* the voice whispered for what seemed like the millionth time, *help.*

"I will," Noah promised as he struggled to his feet.

He continued onward, even if the deeper he got into Genesis, the harder it became to maintain focus. Images drifted into his mind, memories that he had made his own even if they'd never truly belonged to him. When he stumbled into the agora where the Temple of Genesis had once been, the world swirled around him, and he was suddenly in a different time, a different person.

"You remember what you need to do, don't you, Uriel?" Guardian Abigail arranged Uriel's robes, her familiar face set into a scowl. "You recall everything I taught you?"

"Of course, Mother," Uriel replied dutifully. "I will do my best."

She narrowed her eyes at him, as if to say his best wasn't good enough. She didn't actually speak the words, but that look was enough. Uriel suppressed the urge to fidget, knowing such a show of distress would do nothing to please her.

He must have failed to keep his apprehension from showing because she scoffed. "Go. And don't fail me. Don't fail your people."

Uriel swallowed nervously as he stared at the open doorway and the platform beyond. It was the first time he'd tend to his people without his guardian to assist him. In the past, she'd always guided him through it, but now that he was seven, the Council had deemed him sufficiently trained to take over the process on his own. And Uriel didn't feel ready. He felt scared, so scared to stand all alone in front of the crowd.

Nausea roiled through him as he forced himself to step out onto the platform. His vision went blurry, and he tasted blood in his mouth.

Suddenly, Noah was on his knees in the agora, staring up at the glowing sky. For a few moments, he just lay there, struggling to catch his breath. Those memories struck him particularly hard, because they often intersected with his recollections of the day he'd killed the former Council members—including Guardian Abigail.

The memory still brought guilt with it, but not like before, not when he recalled what the purists had wanted to do to Logan and the other cyborgs. In any case, he couldn't think about that now. Uriel's presence was getting stronger, and Noah couldn't let himself lose track of his goal.

He stood once more and steadily continued on his path. He was halfway across the agora when another memory hit him, so hard he couldn't breathe.

The plasma cannon emerged from the ground, immediately targeting the group of cyborgs in the area. Whoever was manning it didn't care about the purist soldiers who had been standing their ground and protecting the Temple of Genesis from Uriel's force. The wave of energy that swept over the agora struck indiscriminately—and it was headed straight for Logan.

If Logan was hit, he'd undoubtedly be killed, and Uriel couldn't allow that to happen. There had already been too much bloodshed, too much loss. Logan was Raze's friend, and even if he hated Uriel, his affection and protectiveness toward Raze meant more than the hatred.

Uriel didn't think about it too much. He launched himself forward, shielding Logan's body with his own. The bolt of energy struck him, and everything went black.

Something inside him snapped. When he opened his eyes, he found himself lying down in the empty agora. There was no sign of the purist soldiers or the cannon. The Temple had disappeared and in its place, a tall glass and steel building rose up toward the sky. A beautiful yet sad sculpture had been erected in front of it, half-metal, half-stone. And Uriel remembered.

He stared at his hands, hands that weren't truly his own, then looked around the barren agora and screamed.

SOMETHING HAD gone wrong. Logan knew it the moment the ground started to shake. Then again, he'd have known it either way. An ominous sensation had haunted him for a few hours now. He trusted Noah, but he also knew his lover had just recovered from a very serious condition. Noah had been shaken when he'd learned of Project Regenesis, and wasn't strong enough to take on such a momentous task. Logan should have never let him go, especially since they didn't have a clear way of stopping this.

It was too late for regrets now, far too late. In the distance, the glow of the vortex turned the darkening sky of dusk into noon. It was beautiful, and yet it scared Logan.

He rushed to the hovercraft he'd managed to find and fix, all the while cursing himself for being a fool. After years of struggling to find a cure for Noah, years of waiting and hoping, how could he have abandoned his lover? The rational part of him reminded him there was nothing he could have done and nothing he *could* do. If he tried to approach Genesis, the vortex would kill him.

But none of those considerations mattered when deep within his heart, he felt Noah needed him. Was he going to his doom? Perhaps. But Noah had been the reason he hadn't stopped fighting after Raze's death. It was why he'd stayed in Zion to begin with instead of leaving with Anne Marie. Noah needed him, and Logan had to go to him.

Of course, it was easier said than done. The hovercraft obediently carried him out of Zion, but by the time he left the city, the vortex had reached the outskirts. The aircraft protested, the controls growing unresponsive even as Logan futilely tried to keep himself from crashing.

The vortex was so close now Logan could feel the electricity in the air. Even if he'd wanted to, he couldn't have turned back now. He braced himself for the blow he knew would come, for the moment when his implants would be turned against him.

It never happened. Instead, as the vortex engulfed both him and his aircraft, the control panels flared to life. Energy sizzled over Logan's skin, but his implants didn't die on him like he had expected.

Maybe he would have rejoiced at that, but he was too busy staring at the image that appeared on his screen. "You shouldn't have come here, Logan," Noah said.

Noah's dark tone told Logan everything he needed to know. "Noah…. Where are you? I'll come get you. You don't have to do this."

His lover's shoulders slumped. "It's too late for that now."

Static crackled on the screen, and Noah's image blurred. Logan's breath caught as he tried to figure out what was going on. "Oh my God, what happened?"

He dreaded the answer to his own question, and he was proven correct when Noah sighed and replied. "Uriel happened. He… he was so scared. I tried to get to him and he… I think he pushed me out of my body."

Once upon a time, Logan had hated Uriel. As the years passed, they'd become good friends, bound together by their shared affection toward Noah and Raze. It seemed unbelievable that Uriel would do something like this, but then again, Uriel wasn't exactly in control of anything now.

"I don't think he did it on purpose," Noah said, confirming his thoughts. "It's… it's worse now. He's in so much pain, Logan. I'm going to try to stop him, but you need to leave."

"You know how to end this?" Logan dared to ask.

"Maybe," Noah replied. "I have a chance. But Logan... even if this does work... I'm not sure I'll be able to keep my promise."

Logan had been afraid of that, ever since he'd heard what Uriel had done to Noah. His lover's consciousness was clearly bound to the vortex. If Logan's theories regarding the vortex were correct—and so far, he had no reason to suspect they weren't—Noah must be the one who was keeping him from suffering a fate similar to that of other cyborgs who'd been caught by Uriel's power.

That meant they were in quite a predicament indeed, and if there was a way to stop Uriel, it would risk not only Uriel's life, but Noah's as well.

Still, Logan wasn't ready to give up hope. "Well, I'm holding you to it, baby," he told his lover. "I won't lose you again."

"Logan...."

"No. You said it yourself. We've been apart for too long. Don't throw your life away because you feel that's the only solution. Remember I believe in you."

The look in Noah's eyes just about broke Logan's heart. Maybe it would have been more merciful to give Noah the forgiveness he needed, but Logan was tired of losing. Just this once, he wanted to be selfish. No matter what other people thought, Noah didn't exist solely to clean up Uriel's messes. Noah deserved happiness too, and Logan had every intention of giving him that. The alternative was unthinkable.

"You're just as strong as Uriel is, baby," he told Noah. "The two of you are anchored together, and that is probably why he pushed you out. But the link goes both ways, and you can fight back."

"I know." Noah bit his lip, as if considering his words. "I was just wondering... if it might not be better this way."

Logan felt lightheaded as he began to understand what Noah had in mind. "You think Uriel might be able to take control of the vortex now that he has your body."

"It's possible, yes. And I can help him. I just... I don't know what will happen after that."

151

"Yes you do." Logan forced a smile he didn't feel and pushed back the panic rising inside him. "You'll come back to me. Because I'll be right there with you, holding you, waiting."

Fortunately, Noah didn't protest further. Logan didn't think he could have maintained his façade if Noah had continued to push. Maybe Noah realized that too, because he smiled. "Okay, Logan."

There was sadness in that small twist of lips, a feeling Logan hated and wished he could wipe away. He told himself he could, no, *would* do it soon. But he also feared what those words meant. Noah's agreement could easily hide resignation, not a promise.

"Wait for me, baby," he insisted. He wanted to say more, to ask Noah not to leave him behind. He wanted to scream that he didn't think he'd be able to bear it. But before he could find a way to put all those emotions into words, the vidscreen went black.

Logan's heart fell, but he kept a tight rein on his fear. The hovercraft was still running. The energy of the vortex hadn't killed him. As long as that remained the case, Noah was out there.

He'd forgotten the number of times he'd made the trip from Zion to Genesis. As a rule, it didn't take more than an hour or so, the time depending on what type of aircraft was used. Now, though, those hours seemed to stretch into ages. Up above, the moon shone in the night sky, but through the filter of the vortex, it looked strangely like the sun. Logan distantly wondered if there was a metaphor there that could apply to his situation. If that was the case, he couldn't see it. He couldn't see much of anything, except the never-ending road, each mile consuming one year of his life.

He almost couldn't believe it when, at last, Genesis was within view. Even more shockingly, Noah was at the gates, waiting for him.

Or so Logan thought until he got close enough, and he realized it wasn't Noah after all.

The hovercraft stopped as Uriel looked up at him. "Hello, Logan. Long time no see."

It was eerie to meet Noah's eyes and see someone else. Nausea and anger swelled inside Logan. Even before, Uriel and Noah had been almost identical, but Logan had always considered them very different. And now, that knowledge was twisted and thrown against him, because this had been Noah. He'd touched that body and kissed those lips. And yet the man in front was no longer his lover.

"Indeed," he replied tightly as he left the hovercraft. "And if you don't mind me saying, I think I would have preferred this little reunion to be under different circumstances."

"I can't exactly blame you," Uriel replied. "Believe it or not, I didn't want this either."

Logan believed him, but that didn't make a difference. "You know you can't do this, don't you? You can't take Noah from me."

"That's the last thing I want. The two of you deserve to be happy." Uriel sounded tired. "I just... I need to find Raze."

That was definitely not an answer Logan had expected. Shit. Did Uriel not realize Raze was dead? If so, fixing this would be more problematic than expected.

"Raze was here with you, Uriel," he said. "He's—"

"I know what happened." Uriel cut him off before he could finish the phrase. "I know what I did. But I need you to come with me. For some reason, it's hard for me to approach the mansion where Raze should be. I think it's because my body is there. You have to go in my stead."

Logan narrowed his eyes. "And if I don't? Wouldn't it be better? You need to return Noah's body, Uriel."

"And I will. I... I just have to see Raze. At this point, there's only one hope I have left—that at the very least, this wasn't all for nothing."

Logan couldn't resent Uriel for that. He understood all too well what it was like to love someone with such abandon. Not to mention that Raze had been his friend. If there was any chance Raze was still alive, Logan had to pursue it.

But he ached, ached with the wish to see Noah. His hands itched to reach out and touch the man in front of him. At the same time, his heart wouldn't let him, because this wasn't Noah.

His thoughts must have been pretty obvious, because Uriel extended his hand toward him. Logan couldn't have shied away if he'd tried, and as Uriel brushed his fingers over his cheek, a burst of energy rushed over him.

It was more powerful than anything Logan had experienced before. Logan could only compare it to what he felt when he and Noah had made love, so long ago.

He'd had moments in past years when he'd feared he'd never experience this unique energy again. But it was undoubtedly there, in this touch that wasn't supposed to mean more than platonic comfort from a man he both cared about and hated. It was there because when their bodies made contact, Logan felt a surge of what he could only define as Noah. Uriel's body went rigid, but he didn't pull away. Instead, he fixed Logan with tormented green eyes.

"Please, remember what I asked."

Logan nodded mutely, and just like that, Uriel slumped against his chest like a puppet with his strings cut. Around Logan, the energy gained a distinctly different feel, more biting, more chaotic. And when those emerald eyes opened, they were Noah's once again.

"I told you it was a bad idea to come here. You're so stubborn."

He tried to sound chastising, but his voice trembled and a crystalline tear flowed down his cheek. Logan kissed it away, and then he kissed Noah, because he couldn't *not* do it, couldn't hold back anymore.

He poured every ounce of love and fear into a lip-lock that might have otherwise been considered unremarkable. Because he didn't try to deepen the kiss at all. Now was not the time. Noah was in pain, the aftermath of Uriel's feelings still clinging to him. Logan held him close, silently telling him that he was there, that they'd do this together. He wished he could assure Noah everything would be all right, but that would have been a lie. At this point, Logan didn't dare to hope for much. He just wanted to stop this before more people got hurt.

When they finally broke the kiss, Logan still didn't let go of his lover. "It's not stubbornness if I'm right."

Noah scoffed. He pulled away from Logan's arms, but he still held on to his hand. "Come on. We have to go back in there and check on what Uriel asked us."

Hand in hand, they entered the city. It was quiet and it looked as abandoned as Zion had been. Logan swallowed around the knot in his throat, but didn't want to address it. Here, the inhabitants hadn't gotten the chance to flee at all. Genesis truly was a ghost town.

Shaking off the glum thoughts, Logan focused on Noah. "What exactly happened?"

"I had a very powerful flashback, and when I snapped out of it, I wasn't me anymore. It's happened before, so in hindsight, I can't be surprised it did now. I guess with Uriel's consciousness loose of his body, he tried to cling to me, with a less than pleasant outcome. But it wasn't necessarily a bad thing. I figured some things out."

For the first time since Noah had entered the vortex, Logan heard a hopeful tone in his lover's voice. "Things? What things?"

"These people, everyone here…. They might still be alive, Logan."

Chapter Eleven

NOAH DIDN'T think he could ever explain what he'd felt and seen when he'd been thrust out of his body. The way he'd taken in information outside his human form wasn't the same, and he had trouble interpreting it. There was a very real cognitive dissonance and for quite a while, he'd felt bereft, like a leaf in the wind.

When he'd managed to get a grip, though, he'd sensed it. There was life here, a life that glowed as brightly as the energy of the vortex. Noah hadn't been able to identify the causes behind this particular development, since the energy wasn't actually his own, but rather Uriel's. But he had hoped that if Uriel stayed in his body, he'd manage to rein in the erratic power.

Logan's arrival had changed that plan, but in a way, Noah couldn't bring himself to regret it. His brother was so scared and in so much pain that he hadn't realized how much he could do. In all likelihood, even using Noah's body as a tool, Uriel wouldn't have been able to reverse the effects of the vortex.

But Noah still had hope. He'd managed to protect Logan from the energy that would have at the very least knocked him unconscious. Therefore, the solution to this lay locked somewhere inside him. He just had to find the key.

Logan gaped at him, his eyes widening in disbelief. "That can't be, Noah. Even if Uriel didn't actually kill them, the people in Genesis would have been unconscious for months. There were a lot of purists here, people with pretty low CCs, but not even they managed to escape."

"I know. It shouldn't make any sense. But that's what I felt. I have no idea how it's possible, but Uriel managed to keep them safe somehow."

Logan scowled. "He didn't seem to think that."

"He didn't realize it." Noah sighed, hating the words on his lips, but knowing they needed to be said. "When he tried to heal Raze, he suffered extreme brain damage. I'm not sure what happened after that, but his subconscious must have taken over somehow."

Logan stared at him, and Noah realized he'd never told his lover about what he'd seen when he'd been in Anne Marie's facility. He'd just kind of assumed Logan knew, but of course, that was stupid, since Logan must have only received bits and pieces of information before Uriel's ill-fated attempt to heal Raze.

"Raze's mental computer was badly damaged. Uriel tried to reboot it. Obviously, it didn't work like he'd have liked."

"Oh." Logan swallowed. "I.... Everyone sort of assumed Uriel was lashing out. I suppose we should have known better. I just.... We found out Odette had shot Raze and then nothing."

Noah couldn't blame his lover for the conclusions he'd drawn, because he knew Logan had seen Uriel's perspective too, and had felt Uriel's pain. "I don't think it really mattered at the time. Besides, I doubt Uriel will hold that against you."

"Of course I won't," Uriel's voice sounded again. "In all likelihood, I might have done it if not for the healing thing."

For a few moments, Noah thought Uriel was speaking in his mind again, but when Logan tensed and looked around, he realized that wasn't the case. Uriel's translucent figure appeared by his side, barely visible, but there. "Apologies about earlier. I... I'm a very selfish person, aren't I?"

"Love is selfish," Logan answered after a moment of pause. "I don't like it, but I understand it."

Uriel's smile was a sad ghost of what it had once been. "Thank you. I don't really know what Noah sensed. It's all a jumble to me, but I'm trying to concentrate."

Logan scowled. "So you don't have awareness of everything that happened throughout the past months?"

"It's hard to explain. I remember some things, but it's like… through a veil. I remember the nuclear missiles."

Noah couldn't believe his ears. "Nuclear missiles?"

Logan tightened his hold on him, as if he thought Noah would run away. "The Chinese Empire decided not to take further chances. Of course, if they'd listened to us, they wouldn't have bothered, because as soon as the missiles approached the vortex, Uriel's energy took control of the targeting systems." He grimaced. "The missiles headed back over the ocean, and for a while, we feared the Empire would find themselves with a nasty nuclear surprise of their own making. Fortunately, they crashed in the middle of nowhere with no casualties."

Noah was horrified. Both Logan and Uriel seemed to have accepted nuclear bombing as an alternative and a possibility. It was obvious how much their perspective had changed compared to Noah's, whose last memories were somewhat less glum, if not terribly hopeful. It also occurred to him that no tech weapon worked here because Uriel was subconsciously defending himself. In that case, Anne Marie had probably intended him to slaughter his brother with a knife. Somehow the thought nauseated him even more.

He realized he'd frozen in his tracks when Logan turned toward him and cupped his cheek. "Noah? Baby, are you okay?"

"Yes, I… it was just a shock."

Logan nodded in understanding. Noah stole a look toward his brother, only to find Uriel gone. "Where did he go?"

"I don't know. Perhaps he can't control his conscious presence, especially not so close to ground zero."

They were indeed approaching the mansion. In fact, they'd already passed Noah's abandoned hovercraft and were halfway across the agora. Noah had been so distracted by Logan's presence he hadn't realized it.

"This is where… it's where I had the flashback," he whispered.

158

Logan said nothing. He picked Noah up with ease and started walking forward, his lips pressed together in an angry line. Obviously, no matter what he'd told Uriel, he wasn't going to forgive that too soon.

In fact, Logan kept stealing glances at him, as if thinking Uriel would worm his way back into Noah when he wasn't watching. It hurt, because it meant another thing had been broken, the frail, precious friendship Logan and Uriel had managed to build. Noah didn't blame either of them, but that didn't make things any better.

It was a relief when, at last, the mansion came within view. The pressure of the energy no longer weighed on Noah like it had before, but he still felt the urgency, perhaps even more acutely than ever. His brother might be trying, but some things not even Uriel could do alone.

That knowledge stayed with him as Logan entered the seemingly abandoned house. It accompanied him as he directed Logan toward the medical bay. Not that he really had to. The feel of the energy in the air provided a direct path toward the source of the problem, a clue Logan could easily trace.

At some level, Noah deemed it too easy, because no matter how much he told himself he could handle this, the fact remained that he wasn't in the least bit ready to face it.

When he saw Uriel collapsed in front of a cyber tube, he couldn't help but release a pained whimper. His brother was twitching, his eyes rolled back in his head, his hands clenched into fists as he writhed on the floor. He looked terrible, pale and withered, like he'd been the one with the cellular degeneration condition. There was blood everywhere, on his face, on his clothes, in his hair. So much blood. He was practically lying in a pool of it, and Noah had no idea what to do.

In complete silence, Logan set Noah down but didn't move away. Noah was thankful for that, because he didn't think he could have stayed upright if Logan had left him. He didn't know how he'd ever believed he could handle this on his own when he so obviously couldn't.

"We need to get him to a doctor as soon as possible," Logan said.

Noah nodded, but he knew, like Logan did, that for the moment, they had no chance of providing Uriel with real medical attention. Moving him was out of the question and no tech would work on him. "We have to find Raze. It will help him get a grip, and maybe we can go from there."

Logan scanned the room, his gaze zeroing in on the cyber tube. It was without a doubt the one Raze had been placed in after the attempted assassination. But it was also open and empty.

Noah shared a look with Logan. "He should have been here. He was here when Uriel started the healing process. Going on the assumption that no one has been cognizant since then…."

"Someone took him. If he'd truly recovered and got out on his own, he never would have left Uriel. Someone took him. But who?"

"Who, indeed."

Noah and Logan turned at the same time, only to see Lucius Hartman standing in the doorway. "Hello, Logan. I'm happy to see you are well. Unfortunately, that might not be the case in the near future."

There were other cyborgs behind him, some of whom Noah recognized from his months prior to cryo. All of them were armed to the teeth, and judging by their stances, those weapons were not for show.

To top it off, the cyborgs he'd seen unconscious in his hovercraft were there too, emotionless eyes set on Noah and Logan. They didn't seem in the least bit put out by the situation, or the fact that Uriel was bleeding out on the floor in front of them. Noah couldn't believe his eyes. Even if he'd felt the presences of the inhabitants of Genesis, he would have never in a million years expected them to ambush him and Logan in the mansion.

"How is this possible? What are you doing?"

Lucius fixed him with a steady, undisturbed look. "Protecting Eden. It's unfortunate, but Uriel's power is best used this way. Genesis has become an impenetrable fortress, and gradually, so will all of Eden."

"You cannot be serious," Logan snapped back. "This place isn't safe for anyone. This energy can kill you."

"It can, but it won't. Our Guiding Light is making sure of that."

Noah looked at Uriel's fallen body, then back at Lucius. "You did something to him. What did you do?"

Lucius arched a brow. "Do you think we have any control over the Guiding Light? That would be nice, but I'm afraid it was just all happenstance."

Anger roared through Noah. "Happenstance. Is that why you left him here alone, on the floor, dying?"

"Actually, no. We left him there because we can't move him. This is one room that does have the potential to hurt us."

Logan took a step forward, positioning himself between Noah and Lucius. "Where is Raze, Mr. Hartman?"

"Raze is still recovering from the attack. I removed him from this facility to ensure he receives the best of care." He turned toward Noah. "In any case, it's a good thing that you're here. We need you to stabilize Uriel's condition and make sure the vortex continues to increase."

"So let me get this straight. You want to keep Uriel alive only so that you can use him as a battery?"

"I suppose you could put it that way."

"He saved your life!" Noah shouted. "Doesn't that mean anything to you?"

"I never would have needed saving if not for him," Lucius snapped back. "I lost twenty years of my life. I lost friends, people I considered family. But that's not what matters right now. I'm a soldier, Noah, and Eden is at war. Empty threats weren't going to keep the rest of the world at bay. But now we hold the power. Not even nuclear missiles can hurt us. I'm trying to protect what little we have left."

Noah supposed the so-called unconscious cyborgs had been guards to watch for any possible intruders. He should have realized their presence was a little too convenient. "Well, if this is your idea of protection, you have a screw loose. Uriel is trying hard not to harm anyone, but at some point, he'll break, and then what will happen?"

Lucius shrugged. "If that had ever become a problem, we would have simply eliminated the vortex by eliminating its source.

But it doesn't seem like this will ever happen now that you're here. You can control the vortex far better than the Guiding Light, so the issue is moot."

Well, things were definitely starting to make sense. The fact that Raze's mother had come for him couldn't be a coincidence. Both he and Logan had been played, and they'd fallen for their game.

"To think I felt sorry for you." Noah laughed to himself. "Don't you even care about Julian? Or did you think your wife would handle that?"

A flicker of something passed over Lucius's face, before it quickly vanished. "Julian is a grown man. He doesn't need me to hold his hand. And he had Logan."

"No, he didn't, not like he, and you, wanted to," Logan replied quietly. "You shouldn't have tried to force it, Lucius. You knew I didn't love him."

Lucius's nostrils flared. "I love you like I love my own son. I didn't get the chance to convince Raze to find a less destructive relationship. But you and Jules could have been happy, if you'd just let go."

Noah had had enough. He had believed something similar once upon a time, but he was tired of people using them, making arbitrary decisions according to their own self-interest and then acting self-righteous about it. He might understand the causes of this whole debacle, but he wasn't about to cling to misplaced guilt over something that wasn't his or Uriel's fault, a guilt that had only perpetuated this state of affairs. Uriel deserved better, and this needed to stop.

Not to mention that at some point, the world had seriously gone insane. Noah had no idea how anyone with a rational mind could have decided to plan their future around the fragile hope that Uriel's psyche wouldn't crack, but it was an idiotic move. It was beyond crazy, and if Noah himself hadn't lived through it, he would have never believed it. And even if he knew what price he had to pay for bringing things to the way they were supposed to be, he would pay it. He just had to hope Uriel would understand him and Logan would forgive him.

"This is going to stop, now," he said quietly. "You don't have the right to make choices for Logan, for me, for Uriel, for Raze. Enough already."

He knelt next to his fallen brother and placed his hand on Uriel's shoulders. Just like before, he felt the presence nudge at his consciousness, but this time, he didn't fight it. He accepted it. And when Uriel's mind slid inside him, he hoped this would be enough, and he prayed Uriel would muster control over his abilities. In the end, there was truly no other way.

LOGAN WISHED he could have been surprised when Noah took Uriel's spirit within himself for a second time. He'd known it would happen, since Noah had presented it as a solution, but that didn't make it any easier to witness.

At first it wasn't obvious. Noah staggered for a moment, releasing Uriel's shoulder. He straightened his back, as if bracing himself for something. Lucius and the other cyborgs were watching, oblivious to the momentous change. "What are you trying to do? You can't heal him."

"No, he can't," Uriel replied from Noah's mouth. "But he would try if he had the ability. He would try to save me. Unlike you."

Lucius's breath caught. "Uriel?"

Noah's lips—or Uriel's, depending on how one saw the situation—twisted into a small, bitter smile. "Hello, Lucius. I don't suppose you ever expected this to happen."

"No, I didn't," Lucius admitted. "But then you always tend to surprise us."

There was fondness in his voice, and Logan hated it, because it wasn't real. It was horrible, ugly, given that Uriel's body still lay on the floor, twitching. He couldn't bear it, had to do something about this since Noah couldn't. He might resent Uriel for taking over Noah's body, but this wasn't truly Uriel's fault. That was one thing that seemed to be a common motif for as long as Logan had known Uriel. Shitty things happening, Uriel trying to solve them as best he could, and ending up blamed for less than satisfying results.

163

He picked Uriel up, half-wondering if his implants wouldn't protest the onslaught of energy. Oddly, it didn't happen. Uriel threw a small smile his way. "Thank you. And I really am sorry."

"I know."

The warmth in his eyes reminded Logan so much of Noah it physically hurt. And it hurt even more when that warmth dissipated into a blank expression. It wasn't because of Logan, since Uriel was turning his attention to Lucius. Still, the dread inside him built up even more, and he felt so helpless he could barely breathe. "Uriel," he choked out.

Uriel didn't acknowledge Logan's discomfort. He took a step toward Lucius, and the air around him crackled with energy. "Let's not play this game, Lucius. For once, let's be honest. It's a mystery for me. You hate me so much, and yet you trusted me to keep you alive. How exactly does that work?"

"It's quite easy. You wouldn't do anything that would cause Raze to hate you. I've always known that, and it was confirmed when, despite the brain damage you suffered, you still kept your power from touching us."

It was all said in a matter-of-fact tone, Lucius taking it for granted without seeing anything particularly special about it. Or maybe he did, but he didn't want to acknowledge it. Who could even tell anymore?

"I don't hate you, Uriel," Lucius added, although he didn't sound like he believed it himself. "I just hate our circumstances."

"You know, it's almost funny. Raze and I thought your presence here meant you'd at least accepted our relationship. I thought you were concerned for me even when Raze was shot. How stupid of me, right?"

"Believe it or not, I did care about you," Lucius replied.

Logan didn't know how Lucius could say that with a straight face, but Uriel shrugged. "I suppose it doesn't really matter. It's not news that I've been set against the world from the moment I was born. There's no reason why you should be any different. That isn't ever going to change. The only people who will ever love me are Raze and Noah, and they deserve better than this." He pinned Lucius with a fierce glare. "You're going to leave this room now and free Raze. You know as well as I do you're keeping him unconscious for no reason."

Logan couldn't help a gasp. "Really? He's alive?"

Uriel nodded, although he didn't turn toward Logan. "I don't know how I didn't see it before. They're keeping him unconscious so he won't try to help me. It's so obvious to me now."

Logan winced and looked at the body in his arms. Of course Uriel could tell now, since he was using Noah's senses coupled with his control over the vortex. It was strange how the knowledge of Raze's possible recovery coupled with the dread of what Raze would find when he opened his eyes. He wished there was something he could do, but even without being told, he realized interfering would bring him nothing. He wondered if Raze would be as horrified by his father's actions as Logan was.

"Do you think I wanted this? I did what I had to do to save Eden," Lucius snapped, as if guessing Logan's thoughts. "He never would have seen things my way."

At that, Logan finally managed to muster a reply. "No, he wouldn't have, and maybe that should have told you something."

"It doesn't matter anymore," Uriel said, and his voice sounded tired. "I always knew things would end like this, one way or another. I was born a weapon. I was treated as a holy prophet. I cannot be a person. I cannot start over. Some things are impossible to forgive, and I don't blame anyone for not being able to let go of the past. I wish Raze hadn't gotten in the way that day, but it was not my choice. I do have a choice now. This is the end. No more fighting. No more pain. The hatred has to die with me."

Uriel threw a glance toward Logan. "Tell Raze I'm sorry. I should have at least said good-bye, but I'm not brave enough. I never was. And... take care of Noah."

Logan nodded mutely. He wanted to say something, anything, to explain that he had treasured Uriel's friendship as well. He wanted to at least promise that Noah would never be alone. But words didn't come, and his reassurance would have been empty even if Uriel had given him the chance to provide it.

What happened next somehow managed to be both shocking and anticlimactic. Uriel's body twitched once in Logan's arms. In front of him, Noah collapsed, not unconscious, but weak. And the energy still buzzing around them faded away like it had never been.

The electricity that was the lifeblood of Genesis returned even as Uriel drew his last breath. Logan said nothing. He knelt next to his lover, allowing Noah to touch Uriel's still form. As Noah mourned his dead brother, Logan looked up and met Lucius's eyes. "I hope you're happy."

Chapter Twelve

URIEL'S FUNERAL was held on a beautiful sunny day that almost mocked the solemnity of the occasion. Raze had been the one to decide the date, though, and no one dared to go against him. These days, few people dared to even talk to Raze. The man had barely spoken since his recovery. For the most part, he ignored his parents' existence and only approached Logan with his plans.

Julian was somewhere in the middle. They'd been close all their lives, but Julian's resentment toward both Uriel and Noah had caused a rift between the two brothers. Still, Julian had shown genuine regret for Raze's pain, so Logan was not surprised when he approached Raze next to Uriel's grave.

"What will you do now?"

"Leave," Raze replied without missing a beat. "There's nothing left for me in Genesis."

"Uriel would want you to stay and continue his work."

Raze released a bitter chuckle. "Well, Uriel's not here right now. He never will be again." He brushed his fingers over the stone that marked Uriel's final resting place. It was a simple grave, made special by the statue looming behind it, a statue Noah had carved. "I can't remain in Genesis," Raze said. "I have too many memories here, memories of him, of us, of the plans we made before everything went to hell. We were going to get married, you know. I asked him, and he said yes. He never even got to wear my ring."

167

No one spoke, and Logan was glad Noah had retreated to his quarters after the funeral. He didn't think Noah would have reacted too well to the conversation.

"When are you going?" Julian asked at last.

"Later today. I have to talk to Noah one more time and make sure he has everything he needs."

"I'll be here for him," Logan offered. "You know that."

Raze smiled weakly. "Yes, but Uriel would have wanted me to do it."

What could anyone say to that? There was palpable grief in Raze's voice, and Logan turned away from his friend, his own memories a heavy burden on his heart.

He took Julian's arm and whispered, "Come on. He needs to be alone for a bit."

Julian bit his lip, obviously not comfortable with abandoning Raze to his grief. When Raze didn't say anything, Julian nodded. Together, they made their way out of the small graveyard and headed back into the mansion.

To be fair, it wasn't a real graveyard as much as it was a garden. They'd all felt it would be better to bury Uriel in a place as close to home as possible, discreet and hidden from the eyes of the public. The mansion was the only true home Uriel had ever had, and Raze had deemed it an appropriate location for Uriel's final resting place. That way, he'd said, Uriel's grave would always have someone to watch over it, even if Raze wasn't here anymore.

The proximity of their destination didn't make the silence between Logan and Julian any less awkward. It was Julian who broke it, with a surprising question. "How's Noah?"

"He was hit hard," Logan explained. "He loved Uriel a great deal, and they didn't have a lot of time together after Noah woke up from cryo. Not to mention all the official formalities he has on his plate."

"You're worried about him," Julian guessed. "Do you think the same—"

He wisely didn't finish the phrase, but he'd still pinpointed one of Logan's worst fears. "The same thing, no. This was... a little specific. And as far as I can tell, a lot of resentment died with Uriel. But yes, I am worried. I can't *not* be worried."

"I'll help, insofar as I can," Julian offered. "I made some mistakes, Logan. I was unfair to Uriel, to Noah, to you. I realize that now. But... I want to help."

Logan wondered what Anne Marie had told him. Julian had changed since the last time Logan had seen him, and he didn't think it had solely been caused by Uriel's death. There was a sadness in him Logan didn't recognize from before, a distinctive feeling of alienation. But no matter how much Logan would have liked to go back to the way things had been, it was impossible.

Even if he and Julian had grown up together, Logan could never forget the way Julian had treated Noah. He supposed the problem stemmed at least in part from Julian's feelings for him. Logan had done his best not to lead Julian on and had always pointed out he loved Noah, but it hadn't been enough. A small part of him would always feel guilty about it. That didn't change the fact that there was a rift between them, one that, at least for now, couldn't be bridged.

Still, despite everything, Logan considered Julian a friend. He squeezed Julian's shoulder and forced a smile he didn't feel. "Thanks. We'll probably take you up on that offer sooner than you think. After all, with Uriel dead, we need to overhaul everything, including the Council, and Noah isn't happy with many of the people who used to form part of it."

Julian grimaced, and Logan knew his friend had understood the reference. "One particular member isn't likely to come back anytime soon, not after what Raze and the Council decided."

"Can you blame Raze for being angry?"

Julian shook his head. "Not at all. I just wish things had been different."

So did Logan, but at this point, he'd take whatever he could get. He couldn't tell Julian the truth, not after everything that had happened and all the pain they'd suffered through. "You and me both," he whispered instead.

They went their separate ways once they reached the private wing reserved for their quarters. Logan headed back to his own rooms. After the day he'd had, he was so tired. He didn't want to think about anyone else except Noah.

He found his lover curled up on the bed, his eyes closed, but his eyelids fluttering rapidly as if in REM sleep. Logan was used to the sight by now. Since the… incident, Noah had been displaying a very distinctive ability to communicate with and control most electronic equipment, and he used it at leisure, with a far greater ease than he had before.

Logan plopped down on the bed next to his lover, and as if on cue, Noah opened his eyes. "Is Raze gone?"

"Not yet," Logan replied. "He said he wanted to talk to you first."

Noah rubbed his eyes tiredly. "To be honest, I think it would be for the best if he departed as soon as possible. I just received a communication from the Iberian king. Supposedly, they wanted to convey their regrets, but I think they were just testing me."

"You don't think…." Logan trailed off, not finishing the phrase because he didn't have to and he knew better than to risk it.

Noah shook his head. "No. I can't imagine anyone was surprised we chose to have a private ceremony for Uriel, and there were so many witnesses to his death that it cannot be questioned. But Eden's safety is in my hands now, and there will be a lot of people who will want to exploit any possible weakness."

Noah was right, and they had known that going in. Sadly, they'd also known there was no other way. Uriel's death had been a sacrifice they'd needed to make for the good of Eden. As a clone, Noah didn't warrant the same type of respect and fear Uriel had managed to muster, but he also didn't carry the burden of the past. It was, in many ways, a compromise, as Eden couldn't afford not having the protection of at least one of the brothers, despite the way it looked to the outside world.

"In any case," Noah continued, "Raze's presence is a complication for everyone, including him. Besides, it's high time he got a break."

He smiled as he spoke, and Logan couldn't help but smile back. Even if they'd taken on a challenging task, Logan truly felt they could do it. They'd been given a second chance too, and no matter what Anne Marie's intentions had been, she had helped Noah. So despite everything, optimism bubbled in Logan's heart, as it always did when he was with his lover.

A knock sounded at the door, interrupting their conversation. Logan got up, already guessing who it was. He opened the door and let Raze in.

His friend looked tired. The day had been very stressful for him, and for good reason. "All packed?" Logan asked.

Raze nodded. "The jet is ready too. I just wanted... I wanted to thank you, both of you. I know this is a sacrifice. Eden is a heavy burden to bear."

"And it's time for someone else besides you to bear it," Logan replied. "Don't worry about us. We'll be fine." In the end, anyone would have an easier time than Uriel, even Uriel's clone and his partner.

Raze hugged him tightly, and Logan responded to the embrace. It was so familiar. He and Raze had been together since they were children. Logan still couldn't believe Raze had recovered from his injury. It was a gift Logan would always be thankful for. Even if Raze left and they wouldn't see each other on a regular basis, their friendship would still be as strong as ever, and that was what mattered.

They broke the embrace when Noah joined them. Raze directed his attention toward Noah, who surprisingly reached over and hugged Raze too. "Take care of yourself. And don't be a stranger."

The hug was brief, but there was no awkwardness left when the two most important people in Logan's life pulled apart. "I won't," Raze said. "We'll keep in touch. You have everything you need?"

"Yes, and since the systems are online again, I can take what I don't have."

The smile on his face was predatory. It really shouldn't have aroused Logan, but it did. In his defense, he and Noah hadn't had much time for one another since Genesis had started to recover. They'd had a lot of trouble reorganizing Genesis's citizens. For a while, Logan had feared Uriel's death wouldn't truly end all the hatred, but as it turned out, many people seemed regretful of the Guiding Light's sad demise, as if they'd finally realized he'd been a person. Either way, it had helped Noah take over. In the end, other than the would-be assassin, Odette—who'd been imprisoned—the most important figures of the revolt, identified through Noah's power, had been exiled, although Noah had made it clear to them that he would not be as merciful if they ever returned to Eden.

But between all that, arranging Uriel's funeral and ensuring Zion and the neighboring cities ran well, they barely had time to breathe. When they turned in at night, they were too exhausted to do more than kiss and fall asleep.

Perhaps Raze realized this, because he squeezed Logan's shoulder and, for the first time that day, grinned. "I'm off. I'll contact you later. Take care."

"I'll lead you to the hangars," Logan offered.

Raze shook his head. "I'll be fine. I have to say good-bye to Julian anyway. And you have Noah to worry about now."

With one last smile, Raze left Logan's room and closed the door. "He's a good man," Noah whispered once Raze was gone. "Maybe it's better things turned out this way."

"Maybe," Logan agreed. That didn't change the fact that for the moment, Logan just wanted to let go of reality and be with his lover.

Noah must have realized this, because he relaxed in Logan's embrace. "And I'm guessing that isn't why Raze decided to leave us alone."

Logan couldn't help a light chuckle, even if, under the circumstances, it might not be all that appropriate. He picked Noah up in his arms, ignoring Noah's frustrated sigh. "I can walk by myself, you know," Noah mumbled.

"I know," Logan answered quietly. "I'm just selfish."

And he was, because Noah didn't like remembering all the times he'd been too weak to even stand. Still, he never truly tried to break away, and even now, he set his head on Logan's shoulder, his protest draining out of him.

"Tired?" Logan asked knowingly.

"I've been catching up on the past five years too. It's... exhausting."

Logan wished Noah wasn't trying to do so many things at the same time, but he understood the reasons behind it. "I take it you're still worried."

"A bit." Noah paused. "I looked into the report over the op you participated in, when Abraham Zion was retrieved."

Logan couldn't help a small wince. That was one of the times he felt he'd truly failed both his lover and his friends. He should have been there sooner, kept the secret from coming out before they were ready for it. During that op, he'd also found out about Project Regenesis, and it would forever be linked to the traumatizing event of the deaths of the former Council members.

Fortunately, Noah was doing better when it came to handling the role he'd played in that particular situation. This time around, he didn't address it at all. "I wanted to ask you something," Noah said. "You don't have to answer. I just…. It's been weighing on my mind."

"Whatever you want," Logan answered as he finally set Noah on the bed. He brushed his fingers over Noah's cheek, wishing he could do more to comfort his lover.

"Is he dead?" Noah asked quietly. "The reports never said."

"I shot him myself," Logan replied. "Why?"

"I don't know." Noah shrugged. "I think maybe... it's still a little hard to reconcile what I knew of our domestic and international political situation with what's currently going on. I feel like two weeks ago, he was a huge threat, and now he's gone."

Abraham wasn't the issue here, not really. Noah was trying so hard, but in the end, he couldn't magically adjust to all the changes overnight, not when he was expected to take over his dead brother's duties. Besides, even with the leaders of the revolt gone, the social dynamic in Genesis remained awkward at best. It didn't help that they couldn't trust anyone, not even people they could consider tentative allies, like Julian and Hugh. The two men had remained in

Genesis, but it was unlikely their relationship with Noah would improve anytime soon. Noah also felt they hadn't done enough to acknowledge the pain Uriel had gone through, but that was a sore point they'd decided to bypass for the greater good—both Eden's and that of their little family.

Logan set his libido's needs aside. He joined Noah on the bed and pulled him close, the hold more comforting than sensual. "Get some sleep. The world will still be here when you wake up. And I always will."

The smile Noah gave him was beatific. "I know. And I also don't want to sleep. I lost five years, Logan. I'm not wasting any more of our time together."

Logan wanted to say that any moment Noah spent getting well-deserved rest was more than justified and recommendable. But Noah was nothing if not stubborn. Before Logan could muster any words that would be remotely convincing, Noah climbed on top of him and kissed him.

Logan's resolve faltered, unable to withstand the feelings buried deep within his heart. As much as he tried to make Noah feel safe, he wasn't similarly reassured. He still woke up disoriented at night and reached for Noah, able to breathe only when he slid his hands over warm skin and tangled his fingers through soft golden hair. Their time was precious, because it had always worked against them.

So maybe he should have put up more protest or insisted on Noah getting some sleep, but he couldn't bring himself to. Instead, he pulled Noah closer and took over the kiss, greedy for Noah's taste, wanting nothing more than to feed his addiction to it, to everything that was Noah.

Noah eagerly parted his lips, granting Logan entrance. Their tongues dueled in a battle neither of them really won, both Logan and Noah equally desperate for each other. Logan drank in Noah's muffled moans, but it did nothing to sate his thirst. It fueled it, fueled the burning ache inside him, the one that never really disappeared and would probably always be there for as long as he lived.

It was a scar on his soul, born the day he'd learned Noah was dying, deepening each time he'd had to cut Noah's hair or administer the serum that had kept him alive. It had branded him the day he'd realized the only way for Noah to live involved him facing his worst nightmare, with Logan still being forced to endure life without him. Every single day spent without Noah had made the wound rawer, the pain more acute. And then Noah had almost sacrificed his own identity for Eden, and that had nearly shattered Logan.

If he'd had any way to prevent all of it, anything to trade that would have wiped away all of Noah's pain, he'd have done it in a heartbeat. And yet, paradoxically, he had no regrets. He treasured that scar because it came with the love he had for Noah.

And Noah knew this, because when Logan finally lost control, he accepted it. He surrendered to Logan's dominance, moaning as Logan rolled them over and covered Noah's body with his own. He wrapped his arms around Logan's neck, holding him tighter than ever before, always tighter, as if he wanted to say exactly what Logan had told him earlier. *I'll always be here.*

Logan kissed him until the need to breathe forced them apart. Then he took a second to gather enough oxygen into his lungs, and kissed him again, and again, and again, until he thought he had enough, but didn't, and he kept going, over and over. But the kisses weren't enough, never enough, so Logan started tearing at Noah's clothing with frantic jerky motions that would have embarrassed him under any other circumstances. As it was, he couldn't really be embarrassed, because Noah wasn't much better off, writhing underneath Logan like a wild thing, desperately trying to get a grip on Logan's too-tight clothes and making whining noises in his throat between kisses. Really, those sounds should have been illegal, because they made Logan lightheaded with desire, scrambled his thought processes, and oh, God, he should be touching Noah more, kissing him more, holding him closer, so much closer.

He didn't know how and at which point they managed to get undressed. It was a battle, both of them grappling and struggling, so hungry for one another they sabotaged their own efforts. Either way, the material of Noah's clothes finally yielded to Logan's strength, seams ripping and buttons popping. He heard something break as Noah managed to toss off his shoes. Logan's garments were even less cooperative, the zippers and buckles stubborn in the confrontation with Noah's fingers. In the end, Noah had to pull away for a brief moment so he could finish this seemingly monumental task. And while it was ridiculously difficult—far more than it should have been—it was more than worth it when he returned to Noah's embrace, and they were skin to skin.

Noah was more than enthusiastic, his earlier fatigue having disappeared without a trace. He zeroed in on Logan's dick and gripped it in a tight fist. Logan groaned as Noah's nimble, slender fingers drew out sinful sensation from him. Electricity crackled between them, Noah's bioenergy dancing over Logan's skin, so familiar, so addicting.

He did some touching of his own, though, Noah's caresses feeding the need instead of sating it. While he could never get tired of kissing Noah, all the naked skin now at his disposal was too tempting for him to linger on one target. He nibbled on Noah's ear and swirled his tongue around the lobe, drawing satisfying gasps from his lover. From there, he traveled down Noah's body. He explored Noah's collarbone and the hollow of his throat, perhaps a little more zealous than would have been preferable since he left several red marks behind. Noah didn't seem to mind. His hold on Logan's dick tightened and his cock nudged against Logan's hip as he gasped, "Logan, please!"

Logan wanted to prolong this, to lick every inch of silken skin and worship Noah like he deserved. In the end, he didn't have the patience. He couldn't resist Noah's sweet cries, not now, not ever.

Those cries gave Logan the strength to free himself from Noah's grip, despite his cock throbbing painfully in protest. He focused on Noah, though, and he crawled down his lover's body, zeroing in on Noah's erection.

Noah's moans rose in volume when Logan gripped the base of his shaft, only to turn into choked whimpers the moment Logan swirled his tongue around the head. Not that Logan was much better off. Shit, he was on the brink of coming just from tasting Noah's precum, with the only thing holding him back being the desire to be inside Noah.

But with the feast that was Noah's body in front of him, who could have blamed him? How could he have ever even attempted to resist this? He might have laughed at that thought if he could have mustered any sort of reaction or emotion beyond the almost unbearable desire—and if his mouth hadn't been busy with a far more useful endeavor.

Instead, his thoughts soon dissipated into a haze of lust, and the only thing left was Noah. Noah's hands landed in his hair, guiding him down, and Logan didn't need further instructions. He alternated gentle licks with stronger, more energetic sucks. He got momentarily distracted by Noah's balls, but judging by the sounds Noah made when Logan rolled them in his mouth, his lover didn't mind his choice one bit. And then Logan returned to Noah's dick and started to bob his head up and down Noah's shaft in earnest. In moments, he had Noah hovering on the edge of climax.

He wanted to tell Noah to go ahead and come, but it seemed his lover had other ideas. All of a sudden, Noah pushed him away. Logan was so dazed and startled that he fell and might have hit the headboard if not for the size of the bed. Still, he was a little taken aback, and that gave Noah time to reach for the lubricant dispenser and climb on top of him. Logan's breath caught and he found himself just lying there, watching as his frantic lover retrieved a generous dollop of the slick liquid, then reached behind himself.

He should have probably helped, but he was frozen, in awe of the beauty of the man above him. Sometimes he had moments when he wondered how he could have been so lucky, and this was one of them. Seeing Noah like that, his face flushed, his pupils dilated, his lips swollen, it was a vision, the most beautiful thing Logan had ever been granted the privilege to witness.

As it turned out, this time around Noah wasn't so happy with being worshiped—if he had ever been. He scowled down at Logan, and although there was no real anger in his expression, Logan got the message loud and clear.

He set his hands on Noah's hips and dragged his lover closer. In response, Noah removed his fingers from his own body and steadied himself on Logan's chest. He positioned his body over Logan's cock and slowly pushed down.

It was Logan's time to groan. When Noah's flesh parted to take his cock, he almost came on the spot. Through some miracle, he managed to hold back, although he tightened his hold on Noah to an extent that was probably painful.

He took a few deep breaths, trying to muster some level of control. Noah's determination sabotaged his efforts. Steadily, Noah impaled himself on Logan's dick, his gaze always set on Logan's face. He didn't say anything, but he didn't have to. His power licked over Logan's flesh, and Logan was lost.

He thrust up into Noah, drawing a choked scream from his beautiful lover. From that point on, they both spiraled into a frenzy of unleashed desire. They moved together in perfect synch, taking pleasure and giving it in turn, the slick glide of naked flesh creating a deeper connection, one that went beyond the carnal.

It felt so good it almost hurt. Their bodies simply fit together, like they always had, and this time, Logan was no longer afraid to take what he needed. He might resent the circumstances of how this had come to pass, but he would never stop being grateful for it. As they moved together in their dance of passion, he wished he had more words, a better way to express how he felt for Noah.

Then again, he didn't have to, because he saw that very same emotion in Noah's deep green eyes. Noah rode him with abandon, and Logan took him harder and faster, but it wasn't just the physical pleasure that guided them. It was the desire to be one, to never have to let go again, to cling to each other and truly believe they would never be separated.

When he was inside Noah, Logan could have faith in their future. And that faith, that love shattered whatever control he'd managed to keep. The crackle of electricity seemed to go beyond his skin, traveling through his flesh into his heart. Yet again, Noah was short-circuiting his soul, and Logan would never have it any other way.

They came together, and their shared orgasm almost drove Logan into unconsciousness. Every inch of him flared to life, every cell buzzing with electricity and bliss, and he embraced it all without letting it overwhelm him. These moments were too precious, and he carved every second in his heart and his memory, branding himself with the sound of his name on Noah's lips, the scent of his sweat and the beautiful fall of his hair. When Noah collapsed in his arms, Logan held him close, whispering soft endearments.

They broke apart because the rapidly drying spunk made the embrace somewhat uncomfortable. Noah managed a sleepy mumble of protest when Logan reluctantly tore himself away. Fondness swelling in his chest, Logan smiled at him and kissed his forehead. "Be right back."

Noah beamed at him and nodded. The faith in that expression humbled Logan, but he reminded himself he couldn't just stand there and gawk at Noah. Instead, he went to the bathroom and wet a washcloth. He was unsurprised when, upon returning to the bedroom, he found Noah already asleep.

Carefully, so as not to wake his tired lover, Logan cleaned him up and covered him with the quilt. A small frown drifted on Noah's face, and Logan heard him mumble his brother's name. He pulled Noah into his embrace and caressed his hair, whispering, "It's okay, baby. It's going to be okay."

Noah settled down against his chest, while Logan simply held him and once again thought how lucky he was. The image of a different man with his lover's face drifted into his mind as he closed his eyes. *Thank you, Uriel. I promise I'll take care of Eden, and of him.*

Epilogue

RAZE'S JET was small, fast, and stealthy, an aircraft they regularly used on infiltration missions. As soon as he left Genesis airspace, he activated the stealth shield and changed directions, heading toward the place that hid his heart's desire.

Soon the ocean greeted him, the blue depths glowing in the sun. When the dark beaches came into view, Raze's mouth went dry. He'd maintained control over his emotions throughout the entire day, but now he couldn't do it any longer.

There was no real reason for his fear. The small house remained a perfect retreat, just as it had been years back, when Logan had cared for Noah. Since then, Logan and Noah had removed all information that had ever referred to it. Raze didn't intend to stay here forever, but for now, it was safe. To make sure, Raze had installed additional sensors and he had plans for a stealth shield. But even if he'd done everything in his power to ensure the secrecy of this haven, he still wasn't satisfied, and he never would be until he reached his destination.

It was a good thing that he could have landed an aircraft in his sleep, because the extent of his distraction could have caused him to crash the damn jet. Fortunately, by some sort of miracle, he succeeded in setting the jet down safely on the beach. He remembered to activate the stealth shield, just in case, and then was out of the aircraft in seconds.

As soon as he entered the house, he forced himself to breathe and calm down. In this particular situation, his agitation would be counterproductive. To a certain extent, he managed, or at least he thought so until he actually entered the room he'd been thinking about the entire day.

Uriel opened his eyes and smiled at him. "How was my funeral?" He'd obviously seen straight through Raze's façade of calm.

"Terrible," Raze replied despite his previous resolve. It was the truth. Even if he'd known Uriel's body wasn't beneath the cold earth, he'd still been shaken. He realized all too well how close Uriel had come to making the lie truth. To this day, they weren't quite sure what had brought Uriel back after his heart had stopped, but whatever it had been, Raze was so grateful for it he would never have enough words to express it. He sat on the chair next to Uriel's bed and took his lover's hand. It was small and frail, the effects of his condition still obvious. Even so, he'd started to recover, to the point that he didn't need the cyber tube like he had in the first few days. It was a little hard to say when exactly he'd regain his full strength, since they didn't have a qualified physician to look him over. But Logan had learned a handful of things since he'd fallen for Noah, and he'd assured Raze Uriel would eventually be just fine. Noah had warned Raze it would take time, but he was just as convinced of his brother's eventual recovery. That was the only thing that had kept Raze from hunting down everyone who'd ever hurt Uriel, and the reason he'd agreed to a relatively tame punishment for the Genesis revolt. In the end, it would be better and safer for Uriel to make sure the political situation in Genesis no longer focused on him at all.

For the moment, Uriel needed lots of rest, appropriate nourishment, and a stress-free environment. But of course, because he was Uriel, he seemed more worried about everyone else than himself. "I'm sorry you had to go through that," he said, reaching out to embrace Raze. "If there had been any other way…."

"Don't worry about me." Raze quickly joined Uriel on the bed before his lover could hurt himself in his zeal to reassure him. "As long as I'm here with you, I'll be fine. Focus on recovering, okay?"

Uriel nodded and relaxed once more. They settled down on the bed, with Uriel curled against Raze. The sound of his steady breath soothed the still open wound in Raze's chest, the one his father had caused when he'd told him Uriel was dead.

"How are Noah and Logan?" Uriel asked after a few minutes.

"Busy," Raze replied. "I'm hoping today they'll get some time for themselves."

Uriel started to laugh, but his amusement turned out to be counterproductive, as his chuckles turned into coughs that rattled his fragile frame. Alarmed, Raze reached for a glass and filled it with water. He rubbed Uriel's back as he slowly gave his lover some of the liquid. Uriel's cough soon subsided, but it left him exhausted and breathing hard.

"I hate this," he mumbled.

"I know," Raze replied, petting his hair. "But you're doing so well, baby. You'll be fine in no time. You'll see."

Uriel didn't reply. His eyes were already closing. He whispered his brother's name, and the small frown creasing his forehead smoothed away in his sleep. Raze hoped no nightmares would follow his lover into slumber, because Uriel needed all the rest he could get. On his part, he wouldn't be at ease until he got Uriel as far away from Genesis as possible. The world needed to believe the Guiding Light was dead, and Raze had every intention of making sure the truth never came out.

"THIS COULD have gone better," Lucius Hartman said as he stared at the stone marked with Uriel's name.

His wife scowled. "You knew Uriel was going to die. He would have died eventually, if not then, any day now."

"I'm not sure that changes things," Lucius replied. He could still remember the pain in Raze's eyes, and no matter how much he'd told himself he'd been right in attempting to safeguard Eden, he realized now all of it was a lie and a mistake. He'd pushed Uriel because it had been easy and he'd wanted revenge, and that was one truth that would always be inescapable.

Perhaps his wife realized this, because she tried to soothe him, in her own twisted way. "You know none of the world powers would have allowed him to live. Gallia had assassins coming before the vortex."

Lucius threw a gaze toward her. "You mean other than you?"

She sighed heavily. "Lucius, you knew who I was before we got married. What would you have had me do?"

"Anything but what you did. I could have accepted anything, Anne Marie, but what you did to Julian… I'll never forgive you for that."

"It was not my intent," she snapped at him. "You know as well as I do that I needed to fake my death. But I did keep the clone alive for as long as was needed for the child to be born. What more could you have asked of me?"

Lucius didn't answer. He had known what he was getting himself into when he'd married a woman he'd been supposed to assassinate. Theirs had always been a romance doomed to fail. But her choice, the way she had framed her death so that a clone had died in her place, had brought their son great pain. Raze hadn't even wanted to talk to her, and Julian…. Learning he was a clone's son— and therefore only a half-brother to Raze—had changed him.

But Lucius hadn't done a better job either. By the end, he'd messed up and broken Raze's heart for a useless vengeance. To this day, he couldn't imagine how he'd been so cruel when he'd only ever wanted what was best for his sons. Distantly, he wondered if one day Raze would become an assassin too. He wouldn't be surprised. Raze hadn't been in the best state of mind when he'd left, and while he wasn't a cold-blooded killer, his grief could change that.

Not wanting to think about the possibility of his son hunting him down for revenge, Lucius shook himself and looked away from the grave. "What will you do now? Your former employers must have found out you're still alive."

"Yes, but with recent developments, my talents and connections have become too important. After all, I was instrumental to saving the world."

"I suppose you were," a voice came from behind them.

Lucius pivoted on his heel, startled. With his implants, he should have detected anyone who could have approached them from behind. Besides, he'd been very careful when he and Anne Marie had decided to come to the graveyard. They'd been exiled from Eden, together with many of those who'd supported them. Coming here had been a risk, but he'd deemed it necessary.

He had a moment when he thought he'd taken a foolish chance, but he relaxed when he recognized his son's voice. "Julian? What are you doing here?"

Julian smiled as he stepped forward from the shadows. "Fixing something. I should have perhaps done it long ago."

Lucius didn't see the phaser. The next thing he knew, he was falling, implants short-circuited by a bolt of energy that would have killed a lesser man. He heard his wife cry out and tried to gather his wits, to reboot his implants.

His son didn't let him recover. With a ridiculous amount of ease, he flipped Lucius on the ground and pinned him there. "Mission complete," he said.

It dimly occurred to Lucius that he'd been worried about the wrong son attacking him. That was the last thought that registered before Julian bent over him and the world went black.

Electrify His Heart

Microchips and Purity:
Book One

By Alana Ankh

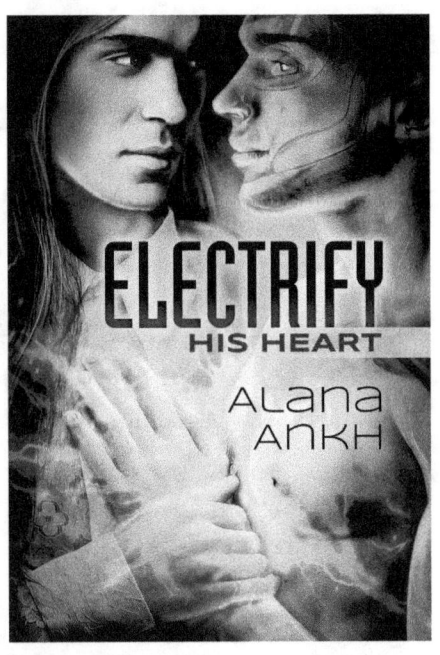

It is the year 2441. A deadly virus has swept over the planet, short-circuiting cybernetic implants, killing billions. In the aftermath, the newly formed state of Eden is led by the one newborn that survived that dreadful day, Uriel Noah of the House of Zion—the Guiding Light. Unbeknownst to all, Uriel lives in a gilded cage, deprived of basic affection, used as a pawn, craving freedom and love.

Cyborg Raze Hartman is the leader of the resistance. His kind—cyborgs with a high cybernetic coefficient—were hit hardest by the virus, the few survivors crippled and enslaved by the purist system. Struggling to keep his father alive, Raze resorts to investigating the Guiding Light, the symbol of cyborg oppression. What he finds changes his life, and Uriel's.

After sneaking into a purist ceremony, Raze sees past Uriel's facade of strength and aloofness. He sees the lonely young man behind the mask of the Guiding Light. The instantaneous attraction between them is literally electric. But a chasm separates them, as wide as the difference between flesh and metal, and the secrets of Uriel's past may be the undoing of them all.

http://www.dreamspinnerpress.com

ALANA ANKH is a hopeless romantic. Once upon a time—no, not in the Stone Ages, but when Alana was a nosy teenager—she lived and breathed mainstream romance, but after she discovered m/m.... Well, her fate was sealed.

Regardless of the genre, Alana thinks love can be painful, heartbreaking, but also fun, corny, and a little silly. Love is different for everyone and anyone—and in her books, she tries to celebrate that.

Alana also loves sci-fi, fantasy, and paranormal. But even if her boys have scales, fur, claws, fangs—or whatever else occurs to her—they're really very nice people. Most of the time. Well.... Most of them are nice, but all of them deserve love and a HEA.

When Alana isn't feeding her addiction to happily-ever-afters and hot men, she's randomly slaying monsters in MMORPGs or thinking up the next idea to share with readers.

Website: http://alanaankh.wordpress.com/
Facebook: https://www.facebook.com/alana.ankh

All's Fair in Mate Bonds and Publishing

By Alana Ankh

For Killian Marsden, werewolf romance is overrated. After all, he should know, since he's a half-werewolf and an editor for a romance-publishing house. He's tired of reading mate bond fairytales, because real life doesn't work that way. In the real world, Alphas abandon their half-breed children. Not that Killian's jaded or anything. Simply realistic. So when werewolf Alpha Brett comes knocking, demanding explanations on a rejected manuscript, Killian reels away, or at least tries to.

Brett is a walking, talking Alpha cliché: big, possessive, and growly. His last name is Wolfe, for crying out loud. But Brett is also trustworthy, devoted to his pack, and a little silly when in love. Soon, Killian discovers that maybe, just maybe, he might love Brett in return.

Unfortunately, Killian is not the only one who wants to claim Brett. He will have to set aside his beliefs about mate bonds and deadbeats if he wants his own happily ever after werewolf romance.

Soul of a Merman

By Alana Ankh

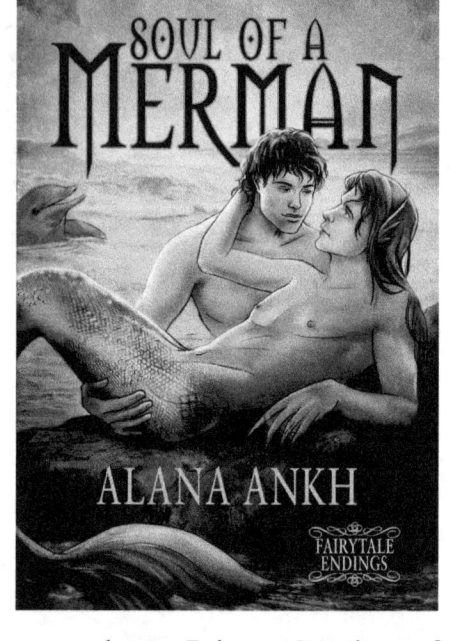

Centuries ago, the sorrow of a spurned mermaid cursed the ocean. Now the fate of the sea rests on the shoulders of her great-nephew, Prince Caspian of Atlantis. Upon inheriting his ancestor's magical voice, he is also entrusted with breaking her curse by finding true love with a human. But Caspian doesn't believe love comes at the swish of the tail, at least, not until he meets oceanographer Stefan Firth.

In spite of the bond that forms between them from the beginning, Stefan's skepticism and his heartbreak over a lost love keep him from even considering a relationship with Caspian. Caspian has no choice but to follow the path his great aunt once did and resort to the Sea Witch's assistance. He must help Stefan love again if he is to break the curse and bring them their fairytale ending.

http://www.dreamspinnerpress.com

Splat!

By Alana Ankh

Splat!

When a small creature has an unfortunate run-in with his car, Deacon Hearst wonders what in the world hit his windshield. A bird? A butterfly? No, that would make Deacon's crazy life too simple. It is a fairy—or rather a Sidhe—with a gaze the color of the moon and thus eloquently named Mooneyes. The little creature's wing is broken, and it's shivering in the rain, and well... Deacon has a heart, after all.

While nursing Moon back to health, Deacon discovers Moon's beauty is more than skin deep. Though they're very different, especially in size, they're alike in their loneliness, their need for affection. Despite the weirdness of the situation, Deacon finds himself falling for his not-quite victim.

Deacon thinks it's a hopeless—gah!—love, but what if it isn't? Moon might just have a few secrets of his own, secrets that could change everything in an instant and weave a different path for them both.

http://www.dreamspinnerpress.com

Beyond the Rift

Elemental Lovers: Book 1

By Alana Ankh

Across the centuries, the Nikari, a race of vicious elemental mages, have built an empire, bringing an entire continent to its knees. The course of history seems set... until one innocent Andari mage changes everything and claims a greater prize—the heart of the Nikari emperor.

Behnivyr 'Ivy' Erethe knows his duty is to wed another Andari Pure-Blood. Craving one moment of freedom before his loveless bonding, he escapes his father's suffocating protection and goes to a masquerade ball, only to unexpectedly meet a mysterious Nikari named Kris. Kris makes Ivy ache with a need he barely dares to acknowledge. One kiss, one dance—and Ivy's life changes forever. Unbeknownst to Ivy, Kris is actually Kristelien Fezenda, the Nikari emperor. Forced to make a difficult choice, Ivy picks love over duty and becomes Kris's concubine.

Poorly prepared for the whirlwind of emotion Ivy summons inside him, Kris now faces the hardest battle of his life. In a ruthless world where all weakness is exploited, where allies become enemies in the blink of an eye, where love can mean death, he will have to defeat more than his own personal demons to breach the rift between him and Ivy.

http://www.dreamspinnerpress.com

Fractured Souls

Elemental Lovers: Book 2

By Alana Ankh

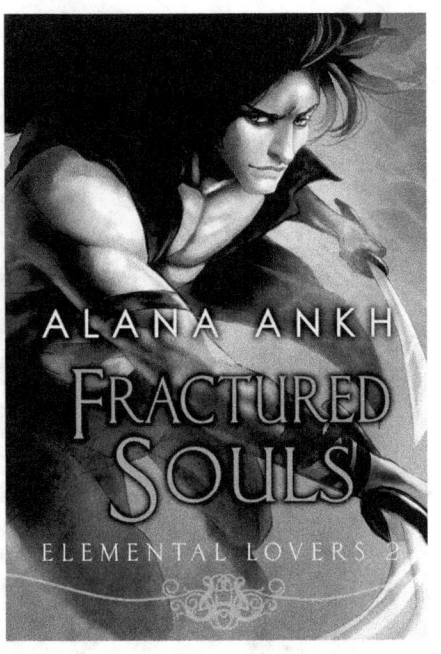

Centuries ago, a group of Aranken mages left their homeland and became the ancestors of the Nikari. Now a Nikari prince will return, seeking truth and finding far more than he expected.

Shuri Fezenda has one goal in mind when he departs for A'rankin—to identify the culprit behind the conspiracy targeting Ivy, his brother's consort and a man Shuri cares for deeply. But when he meets Prince Tynare'Or'Therar, Shuri's world is turned upside down.

Beautiful and mysterious, Tynare draws Shuri like no other. The secrets he whispers taunt and tease, but Shuri's treacherous heart races and his body responds when Tynare shoots him a knowing smile. And then Shuri meets Tynare's twin brother, Nari, and in Nari's kindness and blind eyes, he finds refuge and a love beyond anything he thought he could feel.

Torn between duty and confused emotions, Shuri faces an A'rankin on the brink of civil war and a foe he didn't count on—the neighboring land of Shyrn. At the heart of the conflict, one question remains. Who is Tynare really, and who is Nari? Shuri is almost afraid to learn the answer.

http://www.dreamspinnerpress.com

ALICIA NORDWELL

ADVERSE EFFECTS

SAVING CAEORLEIA

http://www.dreamspinnerpress.com

AN ARGO
NOVEL

NETWORKED

CLAIRE
RUSSETT

http://www.dreamspinnerpress.com